Praise for *Undertow ˘y   )*

Stripped of the unessential, these Hemingwayesque stories reach brilliantly into our chaotic 21st century post-modernism when technology mediates human relationship, the old mores are in dramatic decline, and gender fluidity is on the rise. In rich muscular prose Sgambati illuminates the lingering power of the past, of same sex lovers in a more closeted time, of a teen undergoing sex reassignment, and aging narrators confronting the loss of their physical and mental prowess. Sgambati probes with the humanism of a Junot Diaz the solitary men and women who briefly connect with another and the fleetingness of that connection. "Like the jumpy frames in a silent movie, Owen appeared, then vanished, then reappeared, until the train passed, and then in its wake, we lay tangled and smelling of sex." By turns lyrical, bittersweet, tragic, and celebratory, this is a necessary book that deserves a wide and eager readership.

—Stephanie Dickinson, author of *Girl Behind the Door* and *The Emily Fables*

Vince Sgmbati's collection is a tour through the back alleys of humanity searching for connection. Some of his stories take us through several decades, to watch the unfolding of lives; some capture people in flux or trapped or hidden. His stories are gently told, often in multiple voices, each given the space to tell their side of the story until the sometimes sad and often beautiful picture of people connecting as best they can emerges. It felt like flipping through an old photo album, each image revealed to be much more than it seems.

—tammy lynne stoner, author of *Sugar Land*—IPPY Award and Advocate's Best of 2018

Undertow of Memory will leave you breathless with its subtle beauty and frank, powerful storytelling. You won't want to escape this undertow. You will want to submerge in it, let Sgambati take you to the very special memories that lie in its wake. Each story presents real, complex characters faced with new life challenges informed or haunted by resurfaced past experiences. Aging, loss, transformation, regrets, all the unspoken underpinnings of life receive a voice in Sgambati's masterfully poetic prose. Whether set in a small town or New York City, his stories ignore the bombast of modern life and focus on the whispers of hearts in anguish, seeking resolution. He gives voice to often unspoken emotions making for very powerful storytelling. A triumph of the soft yet potent touch, you will want to revisit the stories and characters in Sgambati's *Undertow of Memory* again and again.

—Gar McVey-Russell, author, *Sin Against the Race*

Also by Vince Sgambati
Most Precious Blood

Most Precious Blood, a finalist in the Foreword Reviews Indies and the Central New York Book of the Year Awards, is set in the eleventh-hour of a declining Italian-American neighborhood where complex and often destructive loyalties have dire consequences. Hard Luck Lenny is the quintessential good son, brother, and father, and he fears a calamity will derail his son's future the way his own dreams were derailed years ago, but Frankie is preoccupied with thoughts of Gennaro DiCico, the son of a small-time mobster. Lenny's fears are realized when a cabdriver's son avenges his father's murder.

Available at amazon.com and guernicaeditions.com

"This book's characters, and their neighborhood, will stay with readers long after they finish it."
—Kirkus Reviews (starred review)

"Sgambati paints a vivid portrait of Italian American life in present day Queens where the past weighs heavier than the present. At once tragic and redemptive, Most Precious Blood is essentially a story of the messy way love, community and family play out and the price we pay for connection."
—Trebor Healey, Lambda award-winning author of *A Horse Named Sorrow* and *Faun*

"...despite the suffering that every surviving character endures, 'permission to live' is the novel's ultimate moral consideration."
—Ezra Dan Feldman, author of *Habitat of Stones*

"Sgambati's often lyrical writing style judiciously sprinkles bits of magical realism..."
—Cardyn Brooks, author of *Dodging Eros*

"Every detail rings true, from the sights and sounds of the neighborhood to the smells of the cooking to the realistic characters."
—Salvatore Sapienza, Lambda Literary award-nominated author of *Seventy times Seven*

Undertow of Memory

Vince Sgambati

Fomite

Burlington VT

ISBN-13: 978-1-947917-35-4
Library of Congress Control Number: 2020930335

Fomite
58 Peru Street
Burlington VT 05401
www.fomitepress.com

To my parents,
Millie and Tony Sgambati

Table of Contents

"We are all just walking each other home."

-Ram Dass

Touching the Elephant

Neither her ubiquitous Long Island accent nor her remarks interested me, but I found myself eavesdropping nonetheless. My eyes rose from my book and there she was at the table next to mine: pretty but unremarkably so, especially under the harsh fluorescence. Had I scanned Bird Library, I might have easily confused her with any number of female Syracuse University undergraduates. I asked her if she was from Long Island, but of course I already knew the answer.

In unison, her friends rolled their eyes, but the young woman smiled and politely answered that she was. Island Park to be specific. She lost her smile when I mentioned the name of a friend, also from Island Park, that I hadn't seen in years.

"Silberman?" she repeated. I wondered if the memory

of a young war bride-turned-widow had caused the young woman's sudden frown. Though, considering her age, it would have been a secondhand memory at best, from stories told by her parents or older neighbors.

"Yes, Maura Silberman," I said. "Maybe you're remembering that her husband, Jimmy, was killed in Vietnam."

"Were there two sisters?" she asked.

"My friend had a younger...." But she cut me off before I finished. Her cheeks flushed, and she said that something terrible had happened to one of the sisters.

I attempted to repeat that Maura's husband had been killed and that maybe she was misremembering, but again she cut me off.

"No, not the husband. Something happened to one of the sisters. My parents are friends with the Silbermans...I mean with Mr. and Mrs. Silberman. If we're talking about the same family. I mean, it's a pretty common name." The girl rambled on, and her friends sat there gaping.

I felt bad pressuring her. She was clearly distraught, but I asked if she might call her parents, to confirm we were talking about the same person.

"Her sister's name is Hannah," I said. "I believe that Mr. Silberman is a dermatologist." I scribbled my name, Rocco Guido, and phone number on a scrap of paper, then told the young woman that I had once been very close friends with the older sister, Maura, and pressed the paper into her damp palm.

Had she been older and the circumstances different, I might have also mentioned Owen, and I might have told her that I met Maura and Owen when I was a freshman at a small college in Vermont, and that although Maura Silberman wasn't the city kid I was, she reminded me of home—loud and gutsy and ethnic—and that Owen West was the Vermont I had envisioned when I lay in my hall bedroom above my grandparents' tailor shop and thumbed through the glossy pages of Vermont Life, not the lonely foreboding place I eventually encountered. She might have understood why a city kid like me—used to the elevated A train passing my bedroom window and streetlights illuminating the nights and delivery trucks greeting the mornings, and crowds of people, as different as the foods they ate and the languages they spoke, poring over dry goods and groceries and fruits and vegetables and fresh flowers and iced fish on sidewalk displays—would have had trouble adjusting to the small Vermont college. The campus, isolated on a hill, looked out on a valley, bordered by more hills: woods, farms, and one modest ski slope. In the valley slept Lyndonville—quaint, picturesque, and imagined by Rod Serling. Maybe the young woman in the library had also had a hard time adjusting to being away from home; she might have been sympathetic, might have understood why Maura and I, two ethnic New Yorkers negotiating the culture shock of Vermont, clicked the way we did. But I didn't share any of this with her, just my phone number and an appeal for more information about Maura.

Later that evening she called me.

It was worse than I feared. Maura had died in a fire. The young woman from the library said that she was sorry about my friend, but that all this gave her the creeps and to please not contact her again. I returned to Bird Library and researched microfiche of Maura's obituary and Long Island newspaper articles mentioning her.

She had remarried and given birth to a daughter. Her baby was two months old when neighbors stood horrified outside of Maura's burning house; her husband was at work. No foul play or carelessness, but an electrical fire caused by faulty wiring. The small, two-story house was already engulfed when fire trucks arrived, and Maura's screams could be heard above the flames' roar. She jumped from a second story bedroom window. Firefighters pried the bundle of wet blankets from out of Maura's charred arms and saved the soaked and shivering but otherwise perfectly healthy infant.

After coming home from the library, downing two Valium, folding myself into a worn, overstuffed chair, and trying to grade papers, a baby's cry filled the shadowy stillness of my bedroom. Smoke, screams, footsteps, water running—maybe the bathtub—then a silhouette darkened my window. My breaths turned shallow; the air felt hot against my skin, and sweat drenched my T-shirt. Finally, the silhouette exploded into flames, then vanished. I replayed these sounds and images over and over, each time slightly altered, but always with the same conclusion, followed by a whisper of a premonition—a sequel to the Vermont story, with Maura's tragic death being the preface. Does Owen know? I hadn't seen him in years. Like the proverbial blind man touching the elephant, I was privy to only a touch, but that touch rekindled a yearning.

———

During my first few weeks as a freshman at Lyndon College, the fall of 1969, something inside of me broke—for whatever reason, be it leaving home for the first time and going from concrete stoops crowded with friends to a landscape with more cows than people or, as therapists would suggest later on, the weight of my own unresolved losses. Feeling empty became my norm. As if I were viewing fellow students through the wrong end of a telescope, they appeared distant, and buildings, trees, clouds appeared flat and wan, merely facades on a studio back lot. Vermont's long winter and the silence and the pitch-dark nights troubled my imagination. Everything felt surreal and pointless.

I first met Maura and Owen late that September.

They were sophomores and had recently become lovers, but Maura had promised to marry her high-school sweetheart from Island Park long before she met Owen, and had planned for the wedding to take place before Jimmy's deployment to Vietnam.

We met during an impromptu game of charades in the dorm lounge, and Maura and I quickly became an unbeatable team. Owen was terrible at the game. I fell in love with both of them. When I was with them, Vermont came alive—a relief of light and color, tasting of maple sugar and smelling of balsam, everything I had imagined it would be. But of course I couldn't always be with them.

That spring, Maura married Jimmy, and soon after, he was deployed to Vietnam. When Maura returned to Vermont, she and Owen resumed their affair.

Though I loved them both, my feelings for Owen had become more than platonic. My grades were in the toilet, swirling around my depression, and come September, instead of returning to Vermont, I divvied my time between classes at St. John's University in Queens, weekly fifteen-minute therapy sessions with a psychotherapist (out of pocket, as I had no health insurance at the time, and fifteen minutes was all I could afford), and helping my grandfather care for my ailing grandmother. He occasionally opened his tailor shop, but mostly he sat beside her in their second-floor apartment, hemming slacks and altering dresses for longtime customers, while she mumbled the rosary and dozed in front of the television. I kept in touch with Maura and Owen mostly by phone.

In mid-February, Maura met Jimmy in Hawaii during his military rest and recuperation (R&R). After the R&R, Maura and Owen's relationship crumbled into combat with transient truces, as if their only strategy for falling out of love was to hate each other. Less than a month after the R&R, Maura phoned me.

"Pops, I'm in Island Park. Jimmy's helicopter was shot down over Hanoi," Maura said.

I still remember the smell of sauce simmering on the stove and my grandfather sitting at the kitchen table drinking espresso and reading the Sunday paper.

"Is he missing?" I said.

"He's dead," Maura answered, the way she might have said it was raining—a statement of fact, with a slight edge of annoyance in her voice.

Owen drove down from Vermont, and we went to the wake together. He stayed in the background, but when I approached Maura she whispered: "Tell him to leave before we have to have another funeral."

Of course Owen didn't listen, and the next day at the military cemetery we stood with scores of others before rows of open, hungry graves waiting to be fed.

Maura returned to college to complete her junior

year, but she refused to speak to Owen. It was a small college, and there was no way for them to avoid each other.

After the R&R, Owen had started to skip classes and often drove the three-hundred-plus miles from Lyndonville, Vermont, to Queens, New York, arrived in the middle of the night, and threw pebbles at my bedroom window. I may have been immune to the sound of passing trains, but I quickly learned to wake to the shower of pebbles against glass.

Since the hallway landing separated my bedroom from the rest of my grandparents' apartment, my comings and goings didn't disturb them, and they'd become accustomed to Owen showing up after they were asleep. They liked him. I never met anyone who didn't.

Affable to a fault, Owen talked to you with his arm wrapped around your shoulder, leaned against you, watched television with his head or feet in your lap. Being guarded with him was like being guarded with a puppy. Short of tethering him, there was little you could do but accept being snuggled and nuzzled and wrestled with. He treated life the same way he treated people—with enthusiasm. "What a day!" "Can you believe it?" "That's amazing!" And it was with this enthusiasm that he had fallen in love with Maura. He had never met anyone like her, just as he had never seen a day as wonderful as the day he was living or a sunrise as awesome as the sunrise he was watching.

After Jimmy was killed, maybe it was guilt that made Maura fall so completely out of love with Owen. At least she said that she no longer loved him.

One night in late spring, three weeks after Jimmy's funeral, I awoke to the familiar sound of pebbles against my window. Owen and I sat on the edge of my bed, facing an angry Malcolm X chastising a stoned Janice Joplin. My bedroom was a tunnel of posters—civil rights and antiwar activists, pop artists, peace signs and antiwar slogans—and my bookshelves housed left-leaning books and magazines and pamphlets that Owen and I would never discuss. Watching the December 1, 1969, televised draft lottery together was the only political act we ever shared, and when my number turned out to be low (lower numbers were called first for the draft) he shouted, "Holy shit!" Closest I ever heard him come to protesting the war.

Owen leaned forward, his elbows on his knees, and his fingers splayed against his forehead.

"She hates me," he moaned.

I didn't respond. I just listened.

"Really hates me," he continued. "I'm not kidding. She said if I bother her anymore, she'll report me for stalking her. Even call the police."

"She wouldn't do that," I said, but I knew she would.

He looked at me as if to say *We're talking about the same Maura, right?*

He continued to grumble about Maura as train lights from the El outside my window strobed my room, to the staccato of steel screeching against steel—a climactic stop, then recommencing, fading, vanishing.

I don't remember how long Owen talked or everything that he said, but at some point I agreed to drive with him back to Vermont and help him pack his things. With just a couple weeks left in his junior year, he insisted that he was done with college—no point in my trying to convince him otherwise. And who was I to lecture him, having spent my freshman year mixing up day with night, playing cards, smoking pot, and plunging into a funk I had yet to climb out of?

Eventually he undressed down to his skivvies, we slipped under the covers in my twin bed, and he continued talking until we fell asleep.

Sometime later, I awoke to the bed shaking. Crouched at the foot of the bed, Owen sounded muffled, as if he were under a pile of debris: "Gonna jump… gonna jump."

I tried getting him to lie down without waking him, but his eyes shot open, wide and fearful. He was soaked with sweat.

"You must have been having a nightmare," I said,

and sat next to him. He collapsed onto my lap and sobbed.

He had dreamed he was jumping from a burning helicopter. "Jimmy didn't make it," he cried. Owen, burning and sweaty, inched up from my lap and slid against my bare chest. He was hard, and immediately my body responded. I heard the call of another train; again, lights strobed my room. Like the jumpy frames in a silent movie, Owen appeared, then vanished, then reappeared, until the train passed, and then in its wake, we lay tangled and smelling of sex.

Except for the sound of our hearts and breaths, we lay silent. I felt more alive than I had ever felt, but I feared that Owen might think this had been a terrible mistake, and he'd be even more depressed.

I whispered, "Owen, are you..." But before I could finish asking if he was okay, he pressed his fingers against my lips. Eventually I fell asleep.

The next morning, I asked him if he still wanted me to drive back to college with him, and he acted surprised by my question.

"Of course," he said. "Why wouldn't I?" I didn't answer.

Driving up Route 7 through Vermont, I spotted patches of snow lingering below evergreens despite it being the last week in April. Detour signs warned of washed out roads. We talked about Maura, about Owen leaving school, about his parents' probable reactions, about us traveling, about him joining the reserves, about my 4F status because of hypertension—which had been a surprise to me. Owen did most of the talking, but I also contributed. Neither of us mentioned Owen's dream or what had happened between us afterward.

Once we arrived, I helped Owen pack—stuffing his dirty clothes into plastic bags, stripping a few posters from the walls, boxing books; he didn't have any records, just a radio—then we loaded up his Volkswagen Beetle.

I visited with Maura while Owen said good-bye to friends. I spotted her reading Philip Roth's Portnoy's Complaint in Vail Manor. She was subdued, as if still wearing the black dress I had last seen her in and holding the folded tri-cornered American flag.

"How are you?" I asked.

"Don't be ridiculous," she answered.

She already knew that Owen was leaving; it was a small college and lately news about him had traveled fast. His behavior—what Maura called his "nuttiness"—drew a lot of attention. If he hadn't left college of his own volition, she believed that he would have been forced to leave. Students had noticed him staring, zombielike, at Maura in the cafeteria or walking to and from classes. There were even stories of him peeking in her first-floor dorm window. Hoping that being embarrassed might change his behavior, Maura had screamed at him to stop stalking her, in front of other students.

I hadn't realized that things had gotten so bad.

"Are you afraid of him?" I asked.

"No, but it's time for him to grow up. What's done is done."

Maura closed her book and we wandered through Vail Manor's rambling hodgepodge of interconnected buildings—several living quarters, barns and carriage houses—once the rural home of Theodore Vail, the founder of the Bell System. What it lacked in symmetry it made up for in aesthetics: leaded mullion windows, built-in window seats and bookcases, balconies and curved staircases, numerous stone fireplaces, stained and shellacked wood trim, wide planked floors, wainscoting, and paneled ceilings. The horse stalls in the carriage houses had intricate ironwork, and the huge barn, though drafty, made for a great theater. In contrast, the recently built campus buildings—utilitarian dorms, cafeteria, library, and gym—brought a gulag to mind, especially in the harsh Vermont winters. In 1973, the same year Maura would die, Vail Manor would also be demolished. Administrators and board members feared it was a firetrap.

On the balcony, surrounding the grandest of several parlors, we found a quiet place to sit, and through the balusters I glanced at the two huge chairs next to the stone fireplace, the only original furniture left in the manor. Rumor had it that Theodore Vail had the chairs custom-made in preparation for a visit from President William Harding Taft, each man weighing more than three hundred pounds. On many cold winter nights Maura, Owen, and I had nestled into one of the chairs—Owen and I pressed close together and Maura curled onto our laps. We discussed everything and nothing, warmed by a roaring fire, and often fell asleep, later waking to a few embers remaining in the fireplace while outside the hint of sunrise turned the sky pink and the snow lavender.

I sat with my legs crisscrossed, and Maura rested her head in my lap. I thought of what had happened the night before with Owen, but I didn't mention it; in fact, we no longer spoke of Owen, or of Jimmy, or of anything that had been but was no more. She updated me on silly campus gossip, I told her what I had been doing in New York City, but we were mostly quiet, and I stroked her hair as if she were a small child needing sleep.

I'll always remember our walk back to the dorm—Maura's arm through mine, her occasional sighs, and the infinity of stars against the velvety black Vermont sky. I told Maura that I loved her. "I know," she said. "I love you too, Pops." A hug then a kiss, and somehow I knew it would be the last time I'd see her.

After driving back to New York City through the night, I stepped out of Owen's Volkswagen in front of my grandparents' shop. Rush-hour passengers climbed the metal steps to the El, a train passed overhead, and Owen had to repeat several times before I could hear him: "I think I'll just drive back home…I have a lot to explain to my folks."

I assumed it would also be the last time that I'd see him too. What's done is done, I heard Maura say.

Weeks after my last trip to Vermont, I'd wake to the sound of pebbles against my bedroom window, but the sidewalk below would be deserted, except for alley cats hunting rats and lone commuters rushing to or from the El. In time, I stopped going to my window, but in my dreams I returned to Vermont: through Vail Manor's shadowy bowels, I meandered, reaching for the cold spots said to be ghosts, snow crunched under my boots and the wintry air burned my nostrils as I ambled across campus or through wooded areas silenced by snow-heavy boughs; through small, grimy towns, I drove along dark, meandering roads, where the sporadic glow from windows made the road that much more lonely. In another dream, a train careened past my bedroom window, and its lights strobed like a pulse, and Owen appeared, then vanished, then reappeared, and our pulses quickened until my room was consumed with light and heat, and the train came to a screeching halt—and drenched in sweat and smelling of my own semen, I awakened.

Like the pebbles at my window, in time the dreams ceased, and I slept through the night more or less undisturbed until a magazine article, or television show about Vermont, or the smell of balsam at Christmas reminded me to remember.

Several years had passed when I received a wedding invitation in the mail: Mr. and Mrs. Floyd Perkins request the pleasure of your company at the marriage of their daughter Vera Emily to Owen Patrick West. I didn't respond.

Soon after I received the wedding invitation, my grandfather died (my grandmother had already passed), and I moved to Syracuse, New York, to enter a master's program and a marriage. The program lasted longer than the marriage. PhD coursework, teaching, a few acquaintances and one-nighters became my life, and then I met the young woman in the library.

——

Picture albums and studio photographs, mostly of Maura, fanned across a glass-topped coffee table, while the Silbermans leaned toward me from the edge of their leather couch, and we sipped iced tea, munched on cheese and crackers, and exchanged polite chitchat. I sat on their plush white living room carpet. More than ten years had passed since I last saw them at Jimmy's funeral, but they looked and acted much the same: Mr. Silberman a little grayer and with a slight paunch, Mrs. Silberman still very chic, and both of them gregarious. They complimented my shorter hair, and Mr. Silberman said that my beard made me look professorial. "Like a rabbi," he laughed. Despite the years that had passed and the grievous circumstances, we fell into an amicable rapport.

They were sorry to hear of my grandparents' passing and of my divorce, but glad to hear that I would soon have my doctorate. Their daughter Hannah had become a lawyer and married a lawyer. Mr. Silberman had recently retired, and he and Mrs. Silberman were toying with the idea of winters in Florida. Finally, we turned to the albums, and the Silbermans alternated narrating each photograph.

After college graduation, Maura had married a childhood friend. The Sillbermans were surprised, but pleased. "It's good for a woman to be married," Mrs. Silberman explained. "Of course, Maura took it very hard when Jimmy was killed in Vietnam—we all did—but she was too young to be a widow."

The pictures showed a much simpler affair than Maura and Jimmy's wedding had been, but Maura looked lovely in a simple summer frock, her thick brown hair in a loose braid, dark glistening eyes, and her mischievous smile accentuating a single dimple.

Her husband was small and serious looking. "He's a hardworking man…a good father," Mr. Silberman said, while Mrs. Silberman lowered her eyes and fingered a loose thread on her sweater as if she were praying.

As we viewed the photographs of Maura pregnant and then with baby Rachel, Mrs. Silberman said, "She was an amazing mother. I never saw such devotion."

"Fiercely protective, like a lioness," Mr. Silberman added. *A lioness that shielded her cub's body with her own*, I thought, but didn't say. We fell silent. Somehow I managed not to cry.

After the photos of Maura with her newborn, Rachel, in the hospital nursery and photos of Rachel's first weeks of life, the Silbermans simply sat back; like two question marks, they curled into the sigh of their leather couch. No mention of the fire, no newspaper clippings, no concluding words. We were quiet as we sipped our iced tea and snacked on grapes or a wedge of cheese.

When I had initially called them, they knew why. "We'd love to see you," they said—Mr. Silberman holding the phone and Mrs. Silberman in the background. They welcomed opportunities to show off their granddaughter. So while we waited for Rachel to arrive, we ceased speaking of Maura and revisited our earlier conversations.

I explained that after my grandmother died my

grandfather seemed lost, and that within a few months he also passed. Not long after his death, I married and moved upstate. The marriage was a mistake, but the move was good. Mrs. Silberman inquired as to how I had come to live with my grandparents. Her question surprised me. I had assumed that Maura would have told them about my parents.

"And you've never heard again from your mother after she left?" Mrs. Silberman asked.

"Never," I answered.

"And your father?"

"We never spoke of him."

I was embarrassed by the questions, but my own story proved to be a perfect segue to discuss Maura's husband, Lenny. He had remarried a year after Maura died, and according to Mrs. Silberman their relationship with him and his wife was cordial but distant. Lenny feared that too much contact with the Silbermans might cause Rachel to become morbid, so Rachel saw her maternal grandparents occasionally, but not nearly as much as the Silbermans would have liked. "To be honest," Mrs. Silberman said, "Lenny was reluctant to have you meet Rachel."

"I don't have to meet Rachel," I said.

But I was relieved when Mr. Silberman responded, "Nonsense! It's no problem at all." I was embarrassed, though, when he reprimanded his wife. "Why would you bring that up, Stella?"

Sounding more surly than apologetic, Mrs. Silberman reminded me of Maura: "I'm sorry. I shouldn't have said anything. We don't begrudge Lenny for remarrying. She's a very nice woman, his wife. Very kind to Rachel. I just don't understand why seeing us more would make Rachel morbid. I don't even mention Maura, unless Rachel asks questions about her." Mrs. Silberman sighed. "I envy you, Rocco. Catholics believe in an afterlife. Don't they?" Without waiting for my response, she said that she wished she could believe she'd someday be with Maura.

Mr. Silberman's eyes darkened: "Stella, stop. What good will this do?" I was relieved when the doorbell rang.

"It must be them," Mr. Silberman said. "Stella, pull yourself together." He rose to answer the door and Mrs. Silberman dabbed at her eyes with a cocktail napkin and smiled.

Following a burst of cold air from the foyer beyond the living room, Rachel ran to her grandmother's embrace and received what had to be a dozen kisses. "Look how beautiful my Rachela is. Bubbie misses you so much," Mrs. Silberman cooed.

My jaw must have dropped. No wonder Lenny didn't want me to meet Rachel. It wasn't just her blond hair and blue eyes or the way her lips curved into a permanent smile, but also the way she carried herself and tilted her head. Except for Maura's single dimple in her left cheek, Rachel was a female image of Owen. But Maura had married Lenny after graduation and Rachel was born sometime after that, at least two years after the last time Maura had seen Owen.

Mr. Silberman introduced me to Lenny, who apologized for his wife's absence.

"Glad to finally meet you." Lenny was very formal, almost stiff. "Maura spoke of you often. Pops, she called you."

I smiled at the thought of it. I was Pops. Owen was West. She called him by his last name. Owen and I got off easy; some of Maura's pet names for friends could be quite colorful.

Lenny introduced me to Rachel as, "Mommy Maura's friend from college." There was nothing morbid about the child. She quickly warmed to me, was very precocious, and clearly crazy about her grandparents.

Even her voice reminded me of Owen, but her spirit was Maura's. Maura's animated expressions, wry comments, and laughter turned walking across campus, playing a game of cards, or even something as mundane as waiting in line in the cafeteria into an unpredictable adventure. No one was spared and nothing was sacred. Rachel was Maura in training: feisty and irreverent.

Lenny was gentle with Rachel and clearly proud of her, taking every opportunity to brag about how well she was doing in second grade and with her piano lessons. A prodigy, he called her.

Neither Maura nor Owen had been particularly musical. I wondered if Lenny was Rachel's biological father after all. Rachel's coloring could have been the emergence of recessive genes and the other physical similarities could have been of my own imagining. Since Maura and Owen, I had compared every other person I met to them and every feeling I felt to what I felt for them or what I imagined they had felt for each other.

On the long drive home to Syracuse from Long Island—after swapping the heavy traffic on the Cross Island for the heavier traffic on the Cross Bronx, and then finally leaving the city and being able to entertain thoughts other than survival—my thoughts drifted to Vermont and to Maura and Owen, from our first game of charades, to our good-byes. As far as I knew, Maura and Owen had never seen each other again after Owen left college, and if that were true, then Rachel couldn't be Owen's daughter. But what if their paths had crossed again, intentionally or by chance? Owen's family lived less than ninety miles from the college. What if Rachel was Owen's daughter and neither of them knew of the other's existence. Didn't they deserve to know?

With help from an acquaintance at the DMV, I learned that Owen still lived in Vermont. And after a bit more research, I also learned that he managed a sports equipment store, and he and Vera had two children.

I booked a room at a ski resort several miles from their house, and after two days of skiing and fretting over how to explain my surprise visit, I sat in the lodge nursing a cup of hot cocoa and massaging my aching muscles—Central New York's ski slopes pale in comparison to Vermont's, and I was feeling the difference. It being Saturday morning, the lodge was packed.

"Okay, so are you guys already hungry?" I knew the voice. Suddenly I was eighteen again, my first time on skis, and Owen was urging me to snowplow: *Bend your knees... more...lean back...further...too far!* We were laughing and I crashed into him and the two of us fell and rolled in the fresh powder, losing our skis and poles and inhibitions. Remembering, I felt happier than I had felt in a very long time.

It took a moment for me to realize I wasn't dreaming or just remembering. The voice was Owen's and he had also recognized me: "Rocco? Is that you? Rocco? Holy crap! I can't believe this."

He had the same creamy complexion that flushed easily in the cold, thick blond hair, athletic skier's body, and blue eyes—as if lit from within—that could be spotted across a room. But he was also different, more confident, and he comfortably carried out his role as dad. His two little boys, obviously twins, fought over something in their packed lunch. Owen separated them, sat them on the bench at my table, and the disgruntled ruffians calmed.

"Now, let me introduce you boys to an old friend from college," he said to the tops of their sweaty heads. "This is Mr. Guido." The boys scrunched up their faces and giggled.

"Excuse me!" Owen said in response, sounding very much like a father or a schoolteacher—but he also smiled, as did I. Mr. Guido must have sounded odd to these two little Vermonters—Luke and Mason West.

Watching Owen unpack their lunches, I felt like Peter Pan returning too late. Owen had grown into an adult, and I felt stuck in my old bedroom above my grandparents' shop, with the A train rattling by, waiting for the sound of pebbles against my bedroom window. But then I saw little Rachel in Luke and Mason and remembered seeing Owen in Rachel. My quest was valid, at least that's what I told myself. If Owen turned out to be Rachel's father, that would mean she also had two brothers.

———

While the boys ate their lunch and blew spitballs through plastic straws, Owen and I summarized the past ten years of our lives. Minutia—at least my summary felt like minutia and bored me in the telling of it. The lodge was crowded and noisy, ski boots thumped against wooden floors, the din of a cafeteria and vending machine racket, and the echoes of scores of competing conversations reverberated against the log walls and expansive windowpanes. Not the rendezvous I had spent hours fantasizing. I could barely hear Owen or myself speak. This wasn't the place to broach the subject of a secret love child, especially with the half-siblings seated across from me.

Owen invited me to dinner. I accepted his invitation but declined another run on the slopes since I was barely able to stand, never mind ski. Back in my room, I spent most of the day reading, grading papers, watching television—anything to keep me from thinking about Owen, Maura, and Rachel.

But later that afternoon, under a hot shower, my thoughts raced. I could remember more vividly the times I had shared with Maura and Owen than anything that had happened since, until the girl in the library—as if for ten years I'd been sleepwalking. Owen hadn't asked why I was in Vermont, and I hadn't offered him any of my rehearsed lies. Why not? And why had I talked to the girl in the library? And why did I just happen to run into Owen at the lodge? My questions, like the hot steam surrounding me, barely formed then dissipated without answers, and trickled down the tiled walls.

———

Modest, but cozy, their house resembled a small country store with all breakables out of reach of the two very active boys. I learned that most of the knickknacks were sewed, crocheted, knitted, woven, painted and glazed, or hot glued by Vera. Quite the craftswoman, she was also an LPN, not to mention wife and mother. She had a wholesome look, not particularly attractive or unattractive.

"It's wonderful to finally meet you," she said. "Owey's told me so much about you."

Owey? I heard Maura laugh.

Our dinner conversation was mostly a replay of the one in the ski lodge, minus the background noise. I had never eaten tuna noodle casserole, and pretended to like it, and I nodded approvingly when Owen mentioned that Vera canned all their vegetables. I was tempted to say, "Well, Owey, you got yourself quite the little woman here," but instead I swallowed my boiled carrots and smiled. Vera took a few sprigs of lettuce then asked Owen to pass the Italian.

Again, I heard Maura laugh. *She means the dressing, not me*, I scolded Maura. For dessert we had bread pudding and green Jell-O with fruit in it.

The twins climbed onto Owen's lap, and I recalled my ten-hour bus rides from the Port Authority in Manhattan to Lyndonville, Vermont, on the winding, snow-covered

Vermont roads. I remembered the bus speeding through the dark Vermont nights and the blur of lit windows.

I thought of Rachel then, and how Lenny had swept her up into his arms when he bragged about her musical talents. Despite their physical differences, she fit in his arms perfectly, and what they shared could never be replicated. Rachel was where she belonged. Who the hell was I to disrupt these people's lives? Luke and Mason had their father. Rachel had hers. If, in fact, Owen was Rachel's biological father, but Maura didn't tell Owen she was pregnant, why should I? As I considered cutting my visit short, Vera stood up from the table and coaxed the boys away from Owen.

"Time for your bath then bed. Say goodnight to Mr. Guido."

I was disarmed by their generous affection—clearly their father's sons. I returned their hugs and taking in the scent of boys coming to the end of a day filled with skiing and running and wrestling, I was overcome with memories.

"Please excuse me, Rocco." Vera said.

The boys charged out of the dining room, and then up the stairs to the second floor.

"Vera is very nice. You are a lucky man," I said, just to say something.

Owen smiled, and we cleared the table and loaded the dishwasher. I discarded my escape plan; this was the first we'd been alone. I mostly complimented Owen about the twins, the house, the meal, and more about Vera. Just polite, if not awkward chitchat.

Owen closed the dishwasher and looked at me, and I thought, *No, Vera, you're the lucky one.*

"She knows," Owen said. I wasn't quite sure what he meant.

"Knows?" I asked.

"Yes, she knows about Maura." He didn't elaborate and I didn't press the issue. In fact, I attempted to change the subject. No more talking, please, I wanted to say—unless you're going to tell me what I want to hear, that that last night in my room meant as much to you as it meant to me; that the memory of it has haunted you the way it haunted me.

But of course that's not what he said.

"After I left college, I tried to stay away from her," he said. "And for a long time I succeeded."

I asked him to stop talking. What had happened between Maura and him was no longer my concern, and maybe it never was. But he ignored my request and continued.

"I hated Maura but finally forgave her, and with the excuse that I had other friends graduating, I went to her graduation."

He wiped his hands on a paper towel, and I steadied myself against the kitchen counter.

Talking to the girl in the library, seeing Rachel, coming upon Owen in the lodge had felt like touches of something greater if not magical. But sometimes once

we have all the pieces and understand the whole picture,
we still don't know what to do next—as if we were better
off never knowing.

Forgiveness

From the mirror over the dresser, a stranger peers at Lena through cloudy eyes. Her scant black hair, gray at the roots, and withered flesh, conjure up memories of ancient Italian donnas pawing vegetables and fruit or sniffing fish from pushcarts along Second Avenue and—more vividly—memories of the crone in South Beach who years ago yelled at Lena and her sister and cousins when they danced outside of her bungalow singing, "When your hair has turned to silver..." She called them dirty little wops, and the very young Lena shouted back, "You have a face like a fried egg!"

Lena lifts a photograph from the dresser: a faded pyramid of family with her grandmother at the crown, embraced by daughters, daughters-in-law, and grandchildren in front of the rambling summer house with its wide screened-in porch and cascading hydrangeas. Her father had rented this house in South Beach, Staten Island, so that the family's women and children could escape the hot flats in Harlem. Husbands and fathers joined them via railroad and Staten Island Ferry on weekends or on Sunday afternoons and evenings after they closed their shops. Her father was a generous man, and she loved him deeply. She spots herself in the photograph and is hard-pressed to reconcile the young girl with big eyes and thick black curls resting her head on her grandmother's aproned knee with the old-timer staring back at her from the mirror.

"Can't be," Lena whispers.

Rosaries, prayer cards, a jewelry box, hairbrush, and toilet articles clutter the dresser. They're all her things, but why are they here and why are they dusted with bath powder? Why are her family photographs displayed, why is she wearing a nightgown, and why is the stranger in the mirror wearing the identical nightgown? But most important, who is this ancient stranger that glares at her so critically?

Lena's Papa will know. He's upstairs. She's not sure why he's upstairs, but she knows he is, unless he's already gone home...but he wouldn't do that...he wouldn't leave her. That much she's sure of. She lifts a robe from the unmade bed and leaves the room that's not her bedroom though it's filled with her things.

———

"Papa... Papa..."

Charlie wakes slowly to his mother's voice, which

sounds distant and frail. It lacks the emphatic tone of the mother who once summoned him home, from up the block or across the street, for dinner or to finish his home-work. On sticky summer nights when teenagers ruled stoops and negotiated pecking orders until all hours, his mother, like many neighborhood mothers—tired of cross-word puzzles, television, or novenas—called out through open windows onto city streets, because they couldn't sleep until their children were home.

"I'm coming Ma," he hears himself reply, but half asleep he's unsure if he's answering the mother calling him home from long ago or the mother in the down-stairs dining room-turned-bedroom. And why is she calling him Papa instead of Charlie?

In the dim light and from his vantage point at the top of the stairs looking down on her, she appears elfin, like a child with progeria.

"Papa, what are we doing here? Let's go home. We don't belong here."

"Shh…you'll wake Rochelle." Charlie calls, then rush-es down the stairs and ushers Lena back into her bed-room directly below Rochelle's. He pulls the French doors closed behind them. Lena's wearing her hearing aids so Charlie speaks softly, but he also mouths his words like a silent movie actor. "You are home."

"Charlie?" Lena stares at him, then looks around her

room. "This isn't a house, Charlie. It's a shop, like Daddy's grocery or Grandpa's butcher."

Not again, Charlie thinks. His parents moved up from Queens ten years ago after his father's dementia became too advanced for his mother to care for him alone. Charlie's partner agreed to have them move in, and for the next year, until a major stroke ended his father's life, Charlie and Michael spent many nights trying to quiet Frank's nightly rants, and deter him from unlocking doors or climbing out windows. They also carried him up stairs to the bedroom, cleaned up his piss and shit, and carpeted the second-floor hardwoods to muffle the sound, so that at least three-year-old Rochelle's sleep wouldn't be disrupted and she wouldn't be frightened. After Frank passed, they'd turned the dining room into a bedroom for Lena—she had difficulty with stairs—and renovated the first-floor half-bathroom into a full bathroom with laundry facilities.

"Ma, this is our house and these are your things."

Lena stands frozen, like the cat Charlie once saved from being crushed on a highway. As with that petrified animal, seconds pass before Lena responds. Slowly she removes her robe and sits on the edge of her bed. "But I don't understand…. You won't leave me…will you, Charlie?"

"Of course I won't leave you, Ma, but please try to sleep. You don't want to wake Rochelle, do you? It's very late. I promise I won't leave you. I'll never leave you."

Charlie pulls the bedcovers up around his mother's shoulders and wishes he could wipe the too-familiar foreshadowing of dementia from her eyes. He recalls his father, crumbled in a recliner with an afghan tucked around him even though it was August. Frank's expression morphed between vacant stares and confusion, like a hologram of mental decline. Rochelle, barely three, had played patty-cake with her grandfather's trembling hand, and occasionally he smiled.

"Promise me, Charlie, you won't leave without me," Lena pleads.

"I promise you, Mom. I'll still be here in the morning and we'll talk like always." Charlie opens the French doors and spots Rochelle at the top of the stairs, her knees tucked up under her chin and her piano fingers clasped in front of her shins. He smiles, ascends the stairs, and strokes her cheek.

"Hey baby… you okay?"

"I guess so. Grandma?"

"Probably had a bad dream, but she's okay now."

"Is Daddy home yet?"

"No, he's working a double shift. He'll be home in the morning."

Charlie follows Rochelle into her room. She climbs into bed and he helps pull up her bedcovers. "Poppy, could you stay with me a little while?"

"Sure, baby." He lies down next to her and with his three middle fingertips traces figure eights on Rochelle's arm, but he feels guilty about leaving his mother alone.

Two weeks ago, while Lena stood at the kitchen counter eating cereal, milk dribbled from the corner of her mouth and down her chin. Charlie asked her if she felt all right and she nodded, but after finishing her breakfast, Lena complained that she was light-headed and wanted to sit in her room. Though Charlie suspected that Lena was suffering a slight stroke or something worse, he didn't call an ambulance. Lena had long feared doctors and hospitals, not to mention nursing homes. In recent years her fears had worsened—just the mention of a doctor's appointment brought on sleepless nights with bouts of diarrhea. "I'm almost a hundred. Leave me alone," she argued.

Charlie followed his mother from the kitchen into the dining room turned bedroom. *Better she should pass sitting in her room, watching a favorite movie with me near by*, he thought.

He had grown up listening to her say, "One mother can care for five children, but five children can't care for one mother. No, they leave it to strangers. Strangers aren't family."

In her room, he helped Lena sit in her rococo tufted accent chair. Lena valued appearance over comfort. He asked if she felt better. She smiled and nodded. He slipped a DVD into a small portable television and thought, *Thank God for Julia Roberts and Sandra Bullock.*

For the next several days, Lena had slurred her words and complained that she was having trouble walking. By day five, she was back to herself, but tonight, with Rochelle's head against his chest, Charlie worries that Lena's sudden onset of confusion might be another little stroke and that Lena will experience first hand what his father had gone through. Transient ischemic attacks are what the doctor called them, and while tracing figure eights on his daughter's arm, Charlie hopes his mother is asleep and not struggling to make sense of her strange bedroom, or fearing that he will leave without her.

———

Unlike the South Beach crone with the fried egg face, Lena enjoys young people. On weekday mornings, when the tweens wait outside her bedroom window for the school bus, Lena watches Rochelle, careful not to rustle the drapes for fear that she might embarrass her granddaughter. It was too late to be the grandmother she had hoped to be, lively and indispensable like her grandmother and mother had been. They were much younger when their grandchildren were born, but Lena and Frank were older when they adopted Charlie, as were Charlie and Michael when they adopted Rochelle.

Slow-moving and precarious, Lena mostly stays out of the way, especially on school mornings when Rochelle storms through the kitchen, grabbing breakfast, her schoolbooks, and her coat. Once Rochelle is outside with her friends, Lena admires her through the lace drapes. Tall and slender, with almond-shaped eyes and a pecan complexion.

"You resemble that singer," Lena repeats at least once a week. "You know who I mean. Whitney something," Rochelle responds with a smile that Lena reads as tolerance. Not that she faults her granddaughter, after all Lena knows that she repeats herself, and her hearing is poor, so she probably misspeaks more often than she realizes. Once, at the dinner table, as Charlie, Michael, and Rochelle debated politics, Lena mused aloud, "I wonder if I'll live to see a woman president?" If only she had stopped there—but no, she then shrugged her shoulders and said, "Who knows? After all, now we have a colored president." The conversation ceased, and she knew she said something wrong, but could barely remember what it was she had said. Later, Charlie berated her for her choice of words. She was confused by Charlie's reaction. She apologized to Rochelle, and as always Rochelle smiled, even gave her a hug, but Lena wasn't convinced that she had been forgiven. By then, she had also forgotten why she was apologizing.

"I think Rochelle might be a little resentful of the attention you give me," Lena often worried to Charlie.

But Charlie dismissed her concern with, "You know how kids are."

So Lena stands near the window in her bedroom and imagines her granddaughter talking to her the way she goes on and on with her friends, the way Lena once went on and on with her sister and cousins—but then the tweens disappear into a yellow school bus, and Lena waves good-bye behind the lace drapes. Her doors open into the kitchen and Charlie sits on a stool at the counter sipping coffee and reading the morning paper.

"Good morning. How are you feeling?" he says.

There's the familiar whistle, like a train entering a tunnel as Lena presses her red fingernail against her hearing aid and adjusts the volume.

"I said….how are you feeling?" Charlie raises his voice.

"Good," Lena answers then hobbles to the pantry.

"What was that all about last night?"

"I don't know. I was a little confused, but I'm fine now. Sometimes I'm more in the next world than this one." With one hand, she carries a box of cereal, and with her other hand, she presses against the top of the kitchen counters. Charlie brings her a bowl, and she rests the box on the counter and grabs two handfuls of cereal, dropping some in the bowl and some on the floor, where Dusty, the family Westie-Poodle mix, laps up his reward. He's learned to stay close to Lena. Next, Lena soaks her cereal with half-and-half.

Charlie chuckles. "Your secret for a long life: half-and-half and chocolate."

"That reminds me," Lena says as she brings a shaky spoon to her mouth. "I'm all out of chocolate."

"Didn't Michael just buy some when he went shopping?"

"All gone." Lena smiles sheepishly.

Charlie shakes his head. "Then you start crying and want to know why you have such bad diarrhea. Your big C is chocolate, not cancer."

Lena nods. Her spoon taps against the bowl until she scoops up the last of the cereal, and carries the bowl to the sink. She opens the dishwasher and slowly removes the clean dishes one at a time, laboriously drying some with a paper towel then stacking them on the counter below the cupboards. After the clean dishes are put away and the dirty ones are loaded into the dishwasher, she'll shower and get dressed, followed by saying rosaries, watching a DVD or two, which she'll mostly sleep through, and reading or doing crossword puzzles. Over the past year or two Lena does fewer crossword puzzles, rereads the same three or four books, and watches the same movies over and over.

"Here, Ma, take your medicine." Lena's startled by Charlie's voice. He hands her three pills, one at a time and she alternates the pills with sips of water. After Dusty suffered a seizure and Charlie discovered a pill on Lena's bedroom carpet, he showed her the incriminating evidence and took charge of dispensing her medicine.

The dog barks, followed by Michael's voice. Lena adjusts what sounds like a train whistle in her hearing aid and Michael joins them in the kitchen.

"Good morning."

Lena looks up from the opened drawer of silverware to Michael's smile. She likes Michael. "Like a second son," she often says. His cheery manner, a quality that Lena suspects makes him a good nurse, put her at ease the first time she met him almost twenty-five years ago. Frank also liked him and they were always hospitable when Charlie brought Michael to their house, even after years passed and Frank began whispering to Lena, "I think they're boyfriends," and Lena told Frank to get his mind out of the gutter. Of course she knew Frank was right, but why talk about such things?

"Good morning," Lena says. She can't help but notice that her son remains silent, busying himself pouring another cup of coffee, even though he never drinks more than one cup at breakfast. But it's none of her business.

"Gonna grab a shower. Got a minute, Charlie?"

Charlie's eyes remain glued to his cup of coffee. "I'll be up soon."

Lena glances at her son. She hadn't noticed or she'd forgotten how much gray had replaced the black in his hair. She dries the perfectly dry silverware.

———

Charlie sits up in bed, reading with his back pressed

against a mountain of pillows when Michael enters the room dripping wet, a towel wrapped around his waist. No need for Charlie to look up. In his mind's eye, he sees.

"I told Rochelle you worked a double shift last night," Charlie says, and then rereads the same paragraph in his book.

As Michael searches the underwear drawer, his towel drops, and this time Charlie's eyes respond, looking over his reading glasses and following Michael's damp back down to the swell of his buttocks—not the young body he explored twenty-five years ago, but Michael stays in good shape and there's something not only appealing but also reassuring about a mature man's body. They haven't made love in weeks, for them a long time.

Where the fuck were you last night? Charlie thinks. *Double shift, my ass.* He finds Michael's silence unsettling. "My mom woke us last night. I think it scared Rochelle."

"Is she okay?" Michael slips on a pair of jeans, but leaves them unzipped.

"I think Rochelle is okay, but something is going on with my mom. She's getting worse you know." Charlie closes his book and Michael sits at the foot of the bed and rests his hand on Charlie's leg. Sunlight catches the dew on Michael's beard and the hair on his chest and arms, blond with tufts of gray.

He leans forward, his hand moving up Charlie's leg.

"I'm sorry," Michael whispers.

"For what?"

"For everything," Michael answers. He presses his full body against Charlie's and Charlie doesn't resist.

———

After Charlie follows Michael upstairs, Lena lifts Charlie's empty coffee mug from the counter and turns it upside down in the dishwasher. She worries that there's a problem between the *boys*. The house is filled with photographs of Charlie and Michael's life together, anniversaries are celebrated, Christmas and birthday gifts are exchanged with a kiss, Rochelle calls the men Poppy and Daddy—there are countless examples that point to the fact that Charlie and Michael are a couple, but Charlie has never discussed this with Lena, at least not in so many words. Lena appreciates the courtesy. She just wouldn't know what to say, so why talk about it?

After several years of Charlie bringing Michael home for visits, including occasional holidays, Lena and Frank stopped asking Charlie if he had a girlfriend or if he hoped to ever marry, and when Rochelle came along they assumed that just Charlie had adopted her. They didn't know that two men could adopt together. Frank would make comments to Lena—sometimes concerned, sometimes cruel—about the *boys*, but Lena was a pro at denial. Twenty years ago, she would have loved for Charlie and Michael to go their separate ways, but now the prospect saddens her.

Her sadness lingers while she showers and dresses, and she weeps as she says her morning prayers. She prays that the *boys* resolve whatever their problem is, and she hopes that she's not the problem.

Moonstruck is a great antidote for sadness, but Lena falls asleep to Cher telling Danny Aiello that he must propose to her on his knees if he expects them to marry.

She wakes to a blank TV screen and the sound of her granddaughter's voice. She feels that familiar pressure in her bowels and fears that she won't make it to the bathroom in time. She opens the bottom drawer of her dresser and removes a pair of disposable adult underpants—utilitarian, bulky, and distasteful to a woman who once sewed lace on her already fancy undergarments. Lena once carefully wrapped the used—damp, sometimes soiled—underpants in a small plastic bag, and then in a larger plastic bag at the bottom of her closet until trash day. But recently Charlie has noticed an odor in her room and discovered the soiled underwear in her dresser, under clean sweaters, slips, and bras. To save her the embarrassment, he trashes without mentioning it.

It takes awhile, but Lena changes her slightly-soiled underpants and this time remembers to wrap the soiled ones in a plastic bag.

She carries her book from her bedroom, and she hears but

doesn't understand what Charlie and Rochelle are saying; unless someone talks directly to her, most conversations meld with crashing silverware, pots and pans, dishes, doorbells and the occasional train whistle from her hearing aid. She smiles and totters through the kitchen, one hand clutching a Belva Plain novel and the other clutching woodwork, counters, and chair-backs.

"All the talking!" She pauses for a moment before leaving the kitchen.

"Hi, Grandma." Rochelle flashes her a quick smile.

"I slept through my whole movie, but it's a long time before I fall asleep at night. I have a lot of rosaries to say before I fall asleep. You think I'm asleep, but sometimes it takes hours for me to say all my prayers." Lena rambles on as she continues her trek into the living room.

In what's become known as "Grandma's easy chair"—next to the fireplace and facing a row of windows along the front of the house—she carefully lowers herself then flops the last few inches into the overstuffed cushions. Dusty sits next to the ottoman that Lena, no matter how swollen her ankles, never rests her feet on—not lady-like.

"What do you want?" she asks the dog. Once Lena puts on her glasses and opens her book, Dusty sulks back into the kitchen, and Lena reads, enjoying what's familiar and perplexed by what's not.

She's asleep when Charlie calls her from the kitchen for supper—her book is on the floor, some of its loose pages strewn across the carpet, and Lena's glasses sit lopsided across her face.

Charlie finds Lena bending over the stray pages. "I'll get them, Ma. I told you not to pick things up. You might fall."

Some months ago, after yanking open the refrigerator door, Lena fell over backward and banged her head on the hardwood floor. While staring up at the kitchen ceiling, she thought of death, how simple it would have been—quick, painless. She scooted along the floor, closed the refrigerator, and then crawled into her bedroom, where she sat on the carpet with her back against her bed for several hours until Charlie came home from work.

Charlie calls Rochelle several times before she finally comes down from her bedroom to join them for supper.

Lena picks up snippets of Charlie and Rochelle's conversation—something about computers and homework and play rehearsal and eat your broccoli.

"Michael's still working the evening shift?" Lena asks.

"Yes." Charlie faces Lena.

"Hopefully, he's not going to work another double," Rochelle adds, but all Lena understands is double, so she fills in the rest.

"Nursing is a hard job," Lena says.

"Not to mention disgusting." Rochelle makes a face to match her comment, and Lena smiles at her granddaughter, even though she's not sure why Rochelle is making such a horrible face or what's disgusting. Maybe the chicken is too dry.

"You're such a pretty girl and you stay so slim," Lena says to her granddaughter.

"And smart too," Charlie adds. "Don't forget the trophy she won for best delegate at the Model United Nations conference last weekend."

Lena doesn't remember the trophy nor does she know what Model United Nations is, but she's become an expert at improvising. "Who knew that we'd have such a genius in our family."

Conversation resumes between Charlie and Rochelle, and Lena takes in bits of food, along with fragments of conversation and banter, but their topics shift too quickly for her to keep up.

Rochelle jumps up from the table, scrapes the remaining food from her plate into the trash, drops the plate next to the sink, and then leaves the kitchen. Next, Charlie stands, carries his plate to the sink, and sets it on top of Rochelle's. "Take your time, Ma. I'll be back down in a few minutes."

Lena remains at the table with Dusty sprawled out next to her, the dog's eyes follow Lena's fork.

———

Charlie's in his bed, staring at the news on television——

something about the Middle East. His thoughts are on Michael, and how their relationship is like a Chinese painting—more blank space than detail. Why did he doubt that Michael worked a double shift? Why the sudden show of affection and passion this morning, when they hadn't had sex in weeks—guilt or some leftover sexual tension after a night of cruising? When Michael had found Charlie and Lena in the kitchen that morning, he'd asked Charlie, "Got a minute?" But later, he never mentioned what it was he wanted to talk about. After sex, Michael fell asleep. Several hours later he awoke, dressed, grabbed a bite to eat, and left for work before Rochelle came home from school. Maybe *Got a Minute?* was simply code for *I'm horny*. Or maybe it turned out to be the wrong time to tell Charlie that they were through.

They'd first met when Charlie volunteered with a local AIDS organization and Michael was a nurse on the same floor. It seems as if they've always been caretakers, but somewhere along the way they forgot how to take care of each other, and Charlie wonders if this happened gradually, like erosion, over time, or if this fault was always there but suddenly shifted. Regardless, caring for a thirteen-year-old and a ninety-eight-year-old under the same roof is all he can handle for now, and he guesses the same is true for Michael. Maybe it's too much for Michael, but Charlie can't worry about that tonight. He turns off the TV, turns off the light, rolls onto his side, and struggles to empty his mind. Around midnight Charlie's bladder calls, and Michael is asleep next to him. No double shift, at least not tonight.

Watching his stream turn the toilet water a pale yellow, he thinks of long-ago Sunday drives in his father's old black Buick, out on Long Island or up to the Catskills where he'd sit fidgeting in pain until Lena urged Frank to pull over and Charlie would relieve himself along side the car, often peeing on the whitewall tiers—small revenge for a kid that hated those pointless Sunday drives.

He tiptoes down stairs to check on Lena and recalls a particularly unpleasant car trip through a tidy Long Island development where all the houses, automobiles, people, and dogs looked alike. Cloned children played on cloned front lawns: boys played catch or basketball, girls jumped rope or played hopscotch.

"See, Frank," Lena had said. "If we lived in a neighborhood like this one, Charlie would have more friends his age."

"What difference would it make?" Frank pointed his chin toward the car window. "He'd still be over there playing with the girls."

"That's not true, Frank," Lena retorted. In the rearview mirror, Charlie caught his mother's pained expression.

He opens the French doors to his mother's room and

remembers another time—he was about Rochelle's age—when it was his mother that said, "If I had a child who was a homosexual, I'd rather he'd be dead."

Lena's head lifts as he opens the door. She holds up her right hand and crystal rosaries dangle from her fingers. Charlie enters the room, dimly lit from a small lamp on an ornate gold-painted desk, and he leans in closely over Lena's bed.

"Are you okay, Ma?"

Lena nods and Charlie kisses her forehead. She takes her son's hand. "Thank you, Charlie. For everything."

Before returning to his own bed, he checks on Rochelle. She's asleep with Dusty curled up at her feet.

As Charlie climbs back into bed, Michael stirs and asks if everything is okay. "Everything's fine," Charlie answers.

He presses against Michael's warmth, drifts back to sleep, and dreams of the summer bungalow his family once rented in legendary South Beach, where his mother used to vacation every summer when she was a girl. He watches fireflies through screened windows and doors as he and his mother sit at an enamel top kitchen table, and Lena sips coffee, inches a plate of homemade doughnuts toward Charlie, and tells Charlie stories he's heard countless times. He's about nine years old.

A boy, maybe five years older, carrying a six-pack of empty soda bottles, opens the screen door to the kitchen.

The door slams, the bottles clink, and Lena and Charlie look at the boy. "Any empties?" he says and grabs a doughnut from off the plate. His dirty blond hair is slicked back except for the curls forming a V on his forehead, his T-shirt sleeves are rolled up above his tanned shoulders, he walks with a slight swagger, and nine-year-old Charlie is mesmerized.

Charlie wakes and briefly recalls his dream. He rests his fingers on the contour of Michael's shoulder. The house is quiet and he hopes that Lena is sleeping peacefully. Slowly, he drifts back to sleep.

———

Lena dreams of the long-ago, rambling summerhouse in South Beach, with the wide, screened-in porch and cascading hydrangeas. Its kitchen is awash with sunlight and curtains sway on ocean breezes to the songs of seagulls and children, as Lena takes a tray of cookies from the oven, sets the tray on a well-worn butcher block, then throws off her oven mitts and searches for the spatula. Charlie, Michael, and Rochelle enter the kitchen glowing and windblown.

"Hi Grandma!" Rochelle smiles her beautiful smile.

"Look what I baked for you while you three were off swimming," Lena says, and with ease she lifts the tray of cookies.

"They look delicious, Grandma. You're the best!" Rochelle hugs Lena and gives her a big kiss.

Forgiveness

Lena wakes and, at first, wonders why she's not at South Beach, but then she remembers where she is and that she's not alone.

"Charlie is upstairs and he won't leave me," she whispers to herself. With one arm over her eyes and her thumb pressed against a rosary bead, she mumbles, "For you and Michael, Charlie, and for Rochelle."

Oxford Avenue Station

The El above Oxford Avenue wept a woman's blood, and slices of her flesh clung to the underside of the train tracks, while heavier chunks gave way and splattered on windshields and bumpers and on two hapless pedestrians. One year after, almost to the hour, Colin Fuller, in his wingtips and Brooks Brothers suit, cradles a bouquet of long stemmed red roses and steps from the outbound A train onto the Oxford Avenue Station platform.

There is no grave for Colin to rest the flowers on. Just short of a year ago, he poured his wife's ashes along the shoreline in Chatham, where seals bobbed in a mirage of ocean gemstones, illuminated by Cape Cod light, and basked at low tide on sandbars that barely broke the ocean's surface—far from the station.

Colin wonders if the woman in the tollbooth thinks it odd that he descended one set of stairs only to climb stairs on the opposite side of the station, as if he changed his mind. But then maybe the woman's been expecting him. Maybe she was working the evening Sheila Fuller collapsed before the inbound A train.

"Collapsed." That's what the police report stated. A woman stood dangerously close to the edge of the platform, said the conductor and several commuters. No scream or leap or flailing arms.

One woman said: "She was there and then she was gone."

Another: "I thought she fainted, and I expected to see her sprawled out on the platform, but she wasn't."

The report quoted numerous people, who all made similar comments, and given that no note appeared in Sheila's tattered, bloodied clothing or at her home or office, "collapsed" became the likely, or at least the most bearable explanation.

It's been years since Colin's been in a train station, and he's never ridden the elevated trains of Queens, Brooklyn, and the Bronx. A car service has long been his mode of transportation, except for extended trips, when he drives his Ferrari to his house in Chatham or his chalet in Vermont. But, for the first anniversary of Sheila's death, retracing her subway trek from their condo in Tribeca to Oxford Avenue, Queens, seemed fitting. Colin stares through the tracks at the traffic passing below.

———

Wednesday is bingo night at Gate of Heaven Church, and Pina wants to get there early for a good seat. Supper must be quick. She examines the produce at Kyung's Vegetable and Fruit Stand and chooses a small head of escarole. There's always fresh garlic and olive oil in her pantry, and she bought several cans of cannellini beans when she last did a big shopping trip. Beans and scarola will be easy to make before bingo. Pina picks off the wilted leaves and hands Mr. Kyung the escarole, keeping a close watch on him so he doesn't rest his stubby pinky on the edge of the scale. She pays, and after he drops the change in Pina's open palm, he points to the red mesh sack hanging from the crook of Pina's right elbow: "You already got a bag. Yes?"

Kyung's insinuation is met by Pina's terse response: "You expect me to eat the escarole after it's been cozying up to my work shoes?"

Kyung shrugs and stuffs the escarole into a paper bag while Pina offers him a halfhearted thank you, knowing that in a day or two they'll again bicker over whether or not to bag a single pepper or zucchini or stalk of broccoli. Small sales might not be worth the cost of a bag to Kyung, but it isn't Pina's fault that she lives alone and unused produce quickly wilts. Pina's children are grown and out of the house, her youngest a grunt in Afghanistan, and there's no husband to warm Pina's empty nest. She threw him out years ago, after she learned he was shtupping a widow up the block. Though neighbors had their suspicions, they never knew for sure who smashed a brick through the widow's bay window, and when they brought the topic up to Pina she simply shrugged her shoulders and said, "The puttana got what she deserved."

Pina climbs the iron steps leading up to the Lefferts Boulevard Station. She'll be home in plenty of time to prepare supper, eat, clean up and leave early for bingo.

———

Heads turn left, toward the rumble of the approaching train. Three teenagers, pierced, inked, and androgynous, stamp-out lit cigarettes, and a young mother with large hoop earrings and lacquered curls scolds her toddler in Spanish. She snatches the toddler's hand, and Colin grimaces, then glances at his Rolex. Like a letter on an eye chart, the blurred "A" on the front of the approaching train sharpens, and the station trembles to the deafening pitch of steel grating against steel.

In his mind's eye, Colin sees Shelia standing too close to the edge of the platform: tall and slender, with a dancer's exaggerated posture, shoulders squared and head erect. There is no mistaking her meticulously bobbed, honey-colored hair. Colin extends his free hand, but she vanishes against the train's silver sheen and graffitied windows. With a swish, the train doors open, and Colin, like the mimes he and Sheila once watched in front of Town Hall in Provincetown, stands frozen on the platform. Not a clown or harlequin, but a

CEO with one hand extended and empty, the other hand clutching red roses.

Pina exits the train and glances at the bouquet. "For me?" she quips as she brushes past Colin, and inhales the tease of his aftershave—light and clean. She smiles. Partway down the steps, she hears Colin's voice: "Excuse me?"

A boy rushes past Pina, almost knocking her down, and she snaps at the back of his torn denim jacket and green spiked hair: "Look where you're going!" She turns, looks up the steps, and her eyes meet Colin's. Pina is no stranger to subway philanderers, but maybe he misinterpreted her remark as flirting: *For me?* were simply kinder words than *Get the hell out of my way before the doors shut.*

Or maybe Pina was flirting. An attractive, well-dressed man with flowers beats an evening of beans, scarola, and bingo. She can turn away from Colin's hazel eyes, and his salt and pepper waves, and the faint lines bracketing the corners of his lips, which suggest that he smiles more often than his expression suggests now, but she can't turn away from the lonely tear that dampens Colin's cheek and disappears under the shadow of his jaw.

"Are you okay?" Pina asks.

"I'm not sure." Colin sits his Brooks Brothers bottom on the grimy step below the platform, his wingtips two steps below that. Having raised three sons, Pina's impulse is to scold him for getting his suit dirty. *Maybe he's drunk,* she thinks. But it was aftershave, not alcohol that Pina inhaled when she brushed past him. *Drugs, probably cocaine*, considering his expensive clothes. Pina takes in his full head of wavy hair; strands of silver catch the dim light. *What if he's really sick?* The tips of her fingernails brush the back of his right hand. "Do you feel sick? Should I call 9-1-1?"

Colin whispers: "She vanished. My wife was standing too close to the edge and she..." Like the phantom Sheila, his words evaporate, and Pina remembers another spring evening, about a year ago, when she exited the same train at this same station after a stop more abrupt than usual. She remembers how commuters slid from their seats, and those standing clung to poles and overhead rings to keep from falling. When the doors opened, screams could be heard from the platform and avenue below, and a transit officer and the conductor advised commuters whose stop was not Oxford Avenue to remain on the train. Within moments, Oxford Avenue was a cacophony of sirens blaring from police cars, ambulances, and fire trucks. Flashing lights illuminated the tracks from below. Pina left the station, and once she reached the bottom of the El's steps, she pushed her way through the crowd and walked home down 104th Street, fingering the rosaries in her pocket and fighting back tears.

Colin struggles to stand, and Pina dismisses her concerns about his being drunk or drugged. She helps steady him.

"Thank you." Colin's hazel eyes stare into Pina's brown eyes, then he traces her face as if trying to remember. Though Pina knows that men find her attractive, she becomes self-conscious of her aquiline nose and full lips—not the delicate features of soap-opera or sitcom stars. "You must think I'm crazy," Colin says. "You might be right."

Colin's comment frightens Pina, but only a little. She's reassured by the talking below them. A rush of commuters ascend the stairs and press Pina against Colin. He raises his voice above the noise of another train arriving on the other side of the station and says, "I believe we're blocking traffic."

Pina blushes, steps away from him, and turns to leave.

"Please don't," he says and gently rests his hand on her arm.

Within moments, the train is a distant rumble, and the commuters that had rushed past them are now waiting on the platform above. As if divulging a secret, Colin whispers: "It's exactly one year since..."

"I know," Pina responds. At least she thinks that she knows, and there's less shame in being wrong than in being cruel.

Colin's eyes widen. His lashes are wet and his eyes sparkle. "Were you there? Did you see?" And though she hadn't really seen, Pina nods.

Colin's hands tremble and his brow dampens. He asks

Pina if she might answer a question that's been plaguing him. "You see the police report seemed inconclusive, and until now I haven't met anyone who actually saw it happen." His voice quivers. "We were happy. At least I thought we were happy, but how much does a husband really know his wife's thoughts or feelings? I don't even know what brought her *here*, and now I can't ask her."

He looks around the stairwell and shakes his head, and Pina is embarrassed by the way her cardigan sweater strains against her breasts, and by the red mesh sack she carries, heavy with work shoes, an umbrella, a tabloid newspaper, and the bag of escarole. She wishes that she had freshened her lipstick or combed her hair before she left work, and she fears that she smells of food and steam tables.

Finally Colin asks: "Did she jump?"

Pina stares at Colin. He resembles the leading men in vintage movies of Hollywood's Golden Era, what the female residents at the nursing home where Pina works would call "dashing." But Pina's more Anna Magnani than Irene Dunne. They'll never meet again. Why not give him the answer he wants to hear?

She recalls the newspaper articles and the gossip and the gruesome songs neighborhood children exchanged about the woman who took several days to go to heaven after being all over Oxford Avenue, and then Pina says: "She fell. She must have gotten dizzy and blacked out. It was a terrible *accident*. Nothing more than that. A terrible, terrible accident. I'm so very sorry."

As if waking from hibernation, Colin inhales deeply, breathing in the perfume of roses mixed with the stench of gasoline fumes and garbage. He looks at the roses and appears confused, as if someone has suddenly placed them in his hands, and he has no idea why or what to do with them, and then he looks back at Pina. "Will you help me with these? I know it's silly, but I'm not very good at this sort of thing. I don't know where to leave them. I bought them for Sheila…well, not exactly."

He reminds Pina of her sons. Men, whether in coveralls or expensive three-piece suits, are just over-grown boys. And they're never more appealing or dangerous than when they're vulnerable and needy. Pina closes her eyes and makes the sign of the cross. Colin smiles, and then Pina opens her eyes and walks back up the steps past Colin. "Follow me," she says.

Commuters stand along the platform, talking or texting; an older man reads a newspaper. Pina lifts the straps of her red sack onto her right shoulder and draws one rose from the bouquet, then tosses it out onto the tracks. "Now it's your turn," she says, smiling at Colin.

Colin follows her example, and they promenade the length of the platform, tossing roses like children in a bridal party. It's dusk and the commuters glance at them, then back toward the twinkling of two distant lights.

"Perfect," Colin whispers to Pina, and she slips her arm through his as they pause in a shadowy section of the platform. Pina takes Colin's hand and together they toss the last of the roses, as if they are young lovers or an elderly married couple or exactly who they are—strangers now feeling a little less lonely. The two twinkling lights brighten and the letter "A" sharpens.

"Your train," Pina says.

"May I kiss you good-bye?" he asks.

Pina's eyes narrow, but then she shrugs. "You're a funny man."

First, Colin plants a peck on Pina's cheek, but then he rests his hands on her shoulders, turns Pina toward him, and presses his parted lips against hers. She returns his kiss as the platform trembles. She's the first to pull away, and the inbound A train doors swish open.

"Hurry!" Pina says, and she gives him a gentle push toward the open doors.

But Colin protests. "I can catch a later train."

"No, go now. I'll be late for bingo."

Colin laughs.

"Please go," Pina says. She feels her neck and cheeks redden and reaches for the rosaries in her cardigan pocket.

The doors close, and through the dirty Plexiglas Colin mouths the words, "Thank you."

"Ciao," Pina whispers, and then watches the roses twirl behind the departing train.

The Luncheon on the Grass

I sat on a park bench along the John Finley Walk—a 1.6 mile elevated promenade above East River Drive with a panoramic view of the Triborough Bridge, Roosevelt Island Lighthouse, and Randalls and Wards Islands. The river breeze tempered the heat, and Luca, my black lab, sat with his hindquarters pressed against my shin, while his nose twitched at the endless parade of canines, most of them bred to amuse rather than run through woods or roll in anything more rank than pot-pourri. One tiny creature—a barrette gathered fur atop its head—stared accusingly at us from a stroller as if to say, *Hard to believe, but my ancestors were wolves.* I smiled and looked down at my guide to summer events and exhibits at the Metropolitan. As I was reading about an upcoming retrospective devoted to the work of the French painter, Eugene Delacroix, a woman's voice startled me.

"Is he English?"

I almost responded, "No, French," but then realized she was asking about my dog, not Delacroix.

She sat in a wheelchair and stretched out her hand—thin and with skin as fine as pale-blue cellophane. A single, ornate, cocktail ring—onyx, surrounded by diamond chips—sat askew on her ring finger. Her fingernails were glossy and well-manicured.

Luca's fur shone and his body wagged. He's accustomed to admiration.

"Yes, an English lab," I said.

Colorless strands of the woman's sparse hair stirred in the breeze. A sudden gust might have scattered them like dandelion seeds.

"I once had an English lab, but blonde," she said. "At dinner parties she held a plate in her mouth until I gave her a treat. She was partial to pâté and caviar."

I said that Luca was more of a kibble kind of guy, and we both chuckled.

"Luca. An Italian name for an English lab?"

"Named for the boy in *Tea with Mussolini*," I said.

She sighed. "Ah...I adore that movie. All those grand British dames in love with Italy."

Another woman crouched behind the wheelchair, adjusting what appeared to be the brake on one of the wheels, but when she stood my enjoyable conversation turned sour. I had first encountered this other woman earlier that morning when she yelled at me: "Scoop your poop!"

I was walking my congenial Luca and my older, capricious schnoodle, Gertrude. More akin to the designer dogs that paraded along the John Finley Walk, and named from a coin toss—heads for Gertrude, tails for Ethel, as in Stein or Mertz. At the curb, Luca spun around like a top and released a coil of steaming stool; however, Gertrude—more dilatory and easily distracted—sniffed, paced, looked around, sniffed again, paced again, looked around again, and if someone passed as she was about to squat, she paused, stared at them suspiciously, and then resumed sniffing and pacing, as if her perfect spot had been sullied.

Relieving their bowels in public and on concrete is disorienting for my country dogs. We were visitors in New York City. I was pet-sitting two guinea pigs named Eleanor and Franklin (both female), a bearded dragon named Judy, and a cat named Seymour while my son, son-in-law, and granddaughter vacationed on Cape Cod.

Back to my initial encounter with the woman now looming and casting a dismal shadow across the wheelchair, its occupant, and me. While Luca and I waited for Gertrude to complete her excretion ritual, a voice came from over my left shoulder, "Scoop your poop!" I turned, and there she was marching up the street with two miniature poodles scampering to keep up with her stride.

"Excuse me!" I shouted, given her distance. She turned her head with the sharpness of a cobra and repeated, this time with more venom, "Scoop your poop!"

Fuck you—a phrase I rarely mutter and only while driving, in response to drivers who behave as if they own the fucking road, and only if I'm alone in my car—becomes a more common part of my lexicon during my annual Manhattan stays, especially when the novelty of big-city life wears thin and amusement becomes irritation. In addition to mumbling the occasional *fuck you,* I also flip the bird at more than a few cabdrivers, who press on their horns as if they are announcing electronic orgasms, and my top lip recedes like a rabid raccoon's at the sight of reckless deliverymen on bikes, especially since I witnessed one hitting an elderly woman crossing Fifth Avenue. The delivery man pedaled off unscathed while I helped the hapless woman to her feet, offered her my starched and pressed white handkerchief to pat her bloodied shin, and we then shared a bench before a bed of blue giant hyssops bordering Central Park until she regained her confidence. I also bought two bags of cashews from the Nuts-4-Nuts street vendor—one for the injured woman. She offered to pay, but I wouldn't hear of it.

As you can see, I'm usually quite affable, but after a few days in Manhattan, and then *Scoop your poop!* coming from a complete stranger who had no cause to think that I would do otherwise—well that sent me over the edge. So as Gertrude, her concentration having been rudely interrupted, resumed sniffing and pacing, I in fact mumbled, "Fuck you," at the self-appointed Poop Nazi who was most likely in search of another dog-owner to berate.

Technically, it wasn't my poop anyway. I'm not in the habit of defecating at the curb, though there was that one time, walking home from a friend's house after a dinner of wholegrain wild rice and legumes, that I, without warning, had to squat behind some uncultivated honeysuckle; however, the Poop Nazi had no way of knowing about that. Also, not only do I always scoop my dogs' poop and only use biodegradable poop-bags, but if there are other turds within close proximity, I scoop them up as well. No self-appointed Poop Nazi was going to soil my self-image.

As Gertrude squatted, I looked away to give her privacy, and noticed the Poop Nazi standing across the street, a few yards short of Lexington Avenue, and waiting for her poodles to relieve themselves. I quickly tore a green bag from its roll, slipped it over my hand, lifted Luca and Gertrude's leavings, and then raced up the street, holding my dogs' leashes with one hand and in the other hand the poop bag, which swung back and forth, resembling a biodegradable green scrotum.

I held it out as evidence, to disprove her erroneous allegation. "You owe me an apology!" I said.

But she only flared her nostrils and sneered up into the sparse canopy of a spindly locust tree. One of the few species of street trees that survive Manhattan's vehicular exhaust, terra concrete, and dog pee—though barely. Her poodles finished their business in the tiny patch of dirt surrounding the tree and growled at Gertrude, who barked while Luca wagged his tail.

Clearly the Poop Nazi had no intention of acknowledging my presence, never mind apologizing, so I shook the green scrotum, and what happened next was hopefully an accident, but the truth is I'm not completely sure. The bag of poop flew from my hand, struck the Poop Nazi's left cheek, and plopped on the sidewalk next to her foot. Our eyes locked in horror while Luca sniffed at the bag, and in an innocent effort to reclaim what was once his, lifted his leg—his ample golden stream showering not only the poop bag, but also the Poop Nazi's white canvas tennis shoe.

Her eyes bulged, her face turned crimson, and she huffed, spun round on the toes of her now-mismatched shoes, and took off without cleaning up after her poodles.

Practice what you preach, I thought, but I tore another bag from my roll. Given what had just happened, it seemed like the civil thing to do, and though I was tempted to shout, *How about scooping your poop?!*, I'm not one to rub someone's nose in it. I tossed the two green bags in the trash, patted Luca's big square head, and gave my dogs treats.

How, in a city of more than eight million people, I crossed paths for the second time in one day with the Poop Nazi is beyond me, but some things are just meant to be, and despite having enjoyed my brief exchange with the gracious woman in the chair, I was now reminded of all that irritated me about Manhattan—impatient drivers pressing on horns, reckless deliverymen on bikes, people either texting and not looking where they're walking or yelling into their Bluetooths, not to mention self-appointed Poop Nazis telling me, "Scoop your poop!"

Oblivious to the daggers flying above her head, my new acquaintance said, "Judi Dench was my favorite in *Tea With Mussolini*, although I also loved Maggie Smith. And of course Cher, more diva than dame, but still marvelous."

She leaned forward, trying to pet Luca, but I knew that the poor woman might tumble out of her chair and fall prostrate onto John Finely Walk before the Poop Nazi would budge, so, being the better person, I stood and approached them. Luca was careful not to bump the woman's hand.

"Winnie and I are about to have a picnic," she said. "Won't you join us?"

Winnie! As in the Pooh, I thought. *Adolf or Benito, but not*

Winnie. No way I could hang that name on the woman who had shouted, "Scoop your poop!"

Luca sniffed around the standing woman's feet, but she stepped aside, probably to protect her change of tennis shoes. Her eyes narrowed, and I considered the invitation. It was odd to have a perfect stranger invite me to a picnic, but I thought that Winnie waiting on me might be the perfect retribution for her having been so rude. *Justice!* I thought—a more palatable word than revenge.

"Thank you, I'd love to." I smiled albeit smugly at Winnie who was busy staring off at nothing.

"Wonderful! My name is Kathryn."

She extended her hand, and I pressed it gently between my thumb and fingers, and said: "Haber…Haber Nuff is my name."

"Let's move into the shade of the park. It will be cooler there," she said. Several gulls that were sitting on the railing along the promenade took wing, until they were gray check marks against the cloudless blue sky. Beneath them a tugboat hauled a garbage barge along the East River. Not an appetizing sight.

Carl Schurz Park includes fifteen acres of lush green between the John Finley Walk and the Yorkville neighborhood of Manhattan. With the mettle of a five-star general, Winnie navigated Kathryn's wheelchair down the concrete path, and then onto a sloping lawn framed by hydrangeas, lupines, coneflowers, and wood lilies, and shaded by the leafy canopies of beech, oak, and aspen. I thought to offer Winnie assistance—at least to carry the picnic basket, given that the handles pressed into the crook of her ample arm while she pushed Kathryn's wheelchair—but Winnie wore competence as if it were armor, and who was I to suggest that she might benefit from a little help. Onlookers, including children, froze. She kicked a stray ball that a toddler had rolled to his parents, and she barely skirted several blankets where, until her arrival, families, couples, and a lone person reading were enjoying the park's serenity. Kathryn jiggled like a bobble-head doll until Winnie paused beneath the shade of a copper beech and locked the brakes of Kathryn's chair. She pulled a handkerchief from her pocket and wiped beads of sweat from her brow and above her lips.

There was no discussion as to whether or not this was a good spot for a picnic. Kathryn said it was perfect. Had Winnie stopped next to a trashcan, my assumption is that Kathryn still would have said perfect. Unlike Winnie, Kathryn seemed civil and amicable.

Winnie removed a plaid blanket from a bag suspended below the wheelchair's handles and spread it out on the grass. She then leaned over Kathryn, and Kathryn locked her thin fingers behind Winnie's substantial neck. Slowly Winnie stood, lifted Kathryn from the chair, and, with surprising care, as if holding someone cherished, she lowered her onto the blanket and patiently waited for Kathryn to steady herself.

Kathryn patted the blanket and asked that I make myself comfortable, which I did, and Luca lay on the grass next to me. Out of her wheelchair, and in the shade, set against the background of foliage and flowers, Kathryn appeared stronger. More delicate than frail. She folded her slender legs beneath her, and as I observed her profile, I saw traces of a once-beautiful woman, a hint of Audrey Hepburn in her face and manner.

"So are you a native New Yorker, Haber?"

"No, I was born in Vermont," I said, and then explained that I'd attended Cornell University in Ithaca, married, and lived in Central New York ever since.

"Central New York?" Kathryn said, displaying a typical New York City response, in which anyplace north of the Bronx is called upstate.

"Yes, the Finger Lakes area of Central New York," I said and patted Luca. "Where this big guy can go about his business hidden in tall grass, without interruption, while I walk my woodland paths under the peaceful canopies of evergreens and deciduous trees that I planted years ago. No rude passers-by."

I shot a glance at Winnie, but she ignored me, opening several containers of sliced cheeses, sliced peaches, orange sections, grapes, and assorted nuts. She arranged the food on a cranberry-colored glass platter, and then cut chunks of baguette and placed them in an oblong sweetgrass basket while Kathryn and I chatted.

Kathryn said: "Born in Vermont and now living in the country. Sounds lovely. As you said peaceful. I used to ski in Vermont—Stowe and Killington. Do you ski?"

I said: "Yes, but now mostly cross-country. Less crowded."

"You don't like crowds or rude people?" Kathryn chuckled. "Then what brings you to Manhattan?"

"My son, son-in-law, and granddaughter are vacationing on the Cape, and I'm pet-sitting." I looked at Winnie as I said *son-in-law,* expecting her to smirk, almost wanting her to, so I'd have more reason to dislike her, but she merely opened a tin of caviar.

"And does your wife also not like crowds?"

"My wife?" I said.

"Yes. You said you were married."

"Divorced. We split up when she found Jesus." Again, I looked at Winnie, but again no smirk. In hindsight, I'd probably mentioned my son-in-law and made the sarcastic comment about finding Jesus in hopes of offending Winnie, even though I had no reason to think it would. After all, she had said "Scoop your poop," not "Burn in hell because your son is queer." I projected qualities onto her that I abhorred, for no other reason than that she had been intrusive—something my son often accused me of, when I told cashiers that they shouldn't wait on customers who are texting or talking on their cell phones, or when I reminded litterers that there are trash cans on almost every corner in Manhattan. Once, while dining at the sidewalk café across from my son's co-op, when a young couple sitting at the table next to me salted their sentences with the F word, I said: "The two of you look like such a nice and intelligent couple, but using the F word so often diminishes you." I explained that I was not opposed to the occasional slip, and that I also indulged, but they were overdoing it. They apologized and blamed their crass language on too many margaritas. I smiled, allowed them their bogus excuse, and went back to enjoying my seared tuna. When I finished eating and was about to leave, I said: "See, you haven't used the F word once since I mentioned it." Fortunately my son wasn't with me or I'm sure he would have told me to mind my own fucking business, which was probably what the young couple thought.

At any rate, I now considered the possibility that Winnie may have just stepped in dog crap once too often, and that I had overreacted to her comment. Maybe she was just impulsive rather than rude. More hasty than Nazi.

She placed the glass platter and basket on the blanket, along with three smaller plates, utensils, and napkins.

Kathryn laughed. "What do you have against Jesus?"

"Nothing," I said. "It was Lydia, my ex, I had the problem with." But I didn't explain why. My son had come out when he was in middle school. Lydia tried to pray the gay away and repeatedly suggested that Aaron go through conversion therapy. When he began mentioning suicide, I filed for divorce, and given Aaron's age the judge allowed him to decide which parent he wished to live with. He chose me.

To change the subject, I commented on the amount of food. "Were you expecting someone?" I directed my question to Winnie, but after a few moments Kathryn filled the silence.

"Yes, we were expecting you. I once lived to entertain. Extravagant dinner parties and intimate soirees. But that was long ago. Now we have these cozy picnics. You never know who your guests might be. Once, in Central Park, our guest was an opera singer from Milan who performed in Tosca at Lincoln Center. Not a lead role, but still. He was a handsome man with the blackest hair and a booming voice…of course. And another time we picnicked with a university professor who was also a tour guide for *The Gay Secrets of the Met*. Not so handsome, but a delightful little fellow. Reminded me of Truman."

"Truman?" I said.

"Yes, Truman Capote. Once a dear friend of mine—

well, until he wasn't, but that was also long ago. And of course Truman loved to party."

I thought that I caught Winnie roll her eyes and wondered if Kathryn might be a little batty, but then I recalled reading about friendships between Capote and high-society women he called his "swans" during Manhattan's Gilded Age. Surely they were all deceased by now. Maybe Kathryn had been the daughter of a swan—more of a cygnet.

"And you? What do you do? Aside from being a wonderful father and grandfather that is," Kathryn said.

"I'm an arborist, and I teach at the College of Environmental Science and Forestry in Syracuse."

"An arborist. I think you're our first. What do you think of that, Winnie?"

Winnie nodded and removed a bottle of chilled prosecco from an insulated pouch.

"Three glasses, Winnie." Kathryn waved her hand, the one with the large cocktail ring, too large for such delicate fingers. She was certainly the personification of a fading swan, and the down fluttering about her head enhanced the image. Whether or not she had actually known Truman Capote was irrelevant.

"Where on the Cape are your son and his family vacationing?" she asked.

"Provincetown. They go every summer. I used to

go with them to help out when my granddaughter was a toddler."

"Oh, I love Provincetown," Kathryn sighed. "We often drove there from our house in Chatham, especially to visit Norman."

"Let me guess. Norman Mailer," I said.

"Well, not Norman Bates." Kathryn giggled. "Autumn was my favorite season in Provincetown. The layers of light are spectacular. Perfect for painting, especially if you're an impressionist."

"Did Monet tell you that?" I joked, given Kathryn's penchant for name-dropping.

"Don't be silly. I'm not that old. And I don't believe that Monet ever went to Provincetown, although Charles Webster Hawthorne, who began the Cape Cod School of Art in Provincetown, was influenced by the American Impressionist William Merritt Chase, who of course was influenced by Monet. So, indirectly, you may be on to something."

Kathryn waved her hand over our sun-dappled fare. "And our picnic is reminiscent of Manet's *Le Déjeuner Sur l'herbe*. Did you know that Manet influenced Monet? Not the other way around. Easy to remember since 'a' comes before 'o.'"

Winnie lowered her eyes as she handed Kathryn and me crystal flutes of prosecco. The corners of her mouth turned up slightly—I'm sure her way of letting me know that Kathryn had just one-upped me.

"All we need is a nude, zaftig woman to complete Manet's painting," Kathryn chuckled. "Might you oblige us, Winnie?"

Winnie's ears turned red.

Through a break in the trees, I noticed that gulls had returned to the railing along the promenade, and I thought of the seagulls in Provincetown and how my granddaughter loved chasing them—her clumsy but precious cherub body spilling over her feet and tumbling into the warm sand, while the sun reflected jeweled ripples on the bay, and the gulls' caws pierced the salty breeze. For a moment, I forgot about the picnic and was startled when Kathryn said, "Winnie, it's your turn to make a toast."

Winnie finally sat, covering much of the blanket.

I expected her to toast to cleaning up after dogs, but instead she said, "To Haber's son, son-in-law, and grandchild."

I was flabbergasted and ashamed. I had accepted Kathryn's invitation to irritate Winnie, and now I was more the curmudgeon than she. That simple toast made her human. I wondered if she had children, grandchildren, or someone to occasionally wait on her—to offer her prosecco in a crystal flute, or at least coffee in a warm mug. I knew loneliness and wondered if there was someone special that Winnie cared for more than she cared about people cleaning up after their dogs or setting out picnics for an eccentric old woman and strange opera singers or tour guides or arborists. But then I remembered how gently Winnie had lowered Kathryn onto the blanket, and I wondered if in fact Kathryn was Winnie's someone special. I had assumed that Winnie was Kathryn's employee, but my son had long ago taught me to question my assumptions.

There was the ping of crystal flutes. "To Aaron, Darius, and Ava," I said.

"May they bask in Provincetown light," Kathryn added.

Winnie patted Luca's head, obviously forgiving the lab; however, she still didn't look at me. *I didn't pee on your damn sneakers*, I thought. She handed me one of the plates, and then prepared a plate for Kathryn without asking what or how much food Kathryn wanted.

Kathryn filled the air with chatter about Manhattan. She spoke of the city long ago, but without the reverence with which older folks often speak of the past. According to Kathryn, Manhattan was as wonderful and terrible a place back in her day as it was now, but for different reasons. When she spoke of things that she no longer did or could no longer do, she was very matter of fact—no echo of regret. As a girl she had flirted with acting on Broadway, but then found flirting with Broadway backers to be more lucrative. In turn, two marriages, but no children by choice, and therefore no grandchildren. "So I just spoil Winnie," she said. "And her silly poodles. Imagine Winnie having poodles."

I looked at Winnie. She chewed, swallowed, and then took another bite of baguette and cheese.

"Why so quiet, Winnie?" Kathryn said. "By now you are usually complaining about someone talking on a cell phone and not paying attention to a child or someone not cleaning up after a dog."

I stifled a chuckle, but it was also becoming apparent that I had more in common with Winnie than I cared to admit.

Winnie poured Kathryn another glass of prosecco—her not-so-subtle way of telling Kathryn to shut up and drink, but it didn't work. Winnie seemed to be a woman of few words, unless it was my presence that left her mute.

"Why don't you tell Haber about the time the delivery-man sped by on his bicycle?"

But Kathryn didn't give Winnie the chance to explain, not that Winnie would have. Punctuated with bursts of laughter, Kathryn elaborated: "To avoid rear-ending a taxicab, which had stopped to pick up a passenger, he slammed on his brakes, skidded, and his General Tso's chicken, broccoli with garlic sauce, and shrimp lo mein went airborne, and then splattered across the cab's trunk as if it were a Jackson Pollock canvas." While retelling this story,

Kathryn laughed so hard that a few drops of her prosecco spattered the blanket.

Winnie cracked a smile. "That was a good one," she said.

"Winnie is not fond of deliverymen or cabdrivers. Once another deliveryman on a bicycle nearly sideswiped my wheelchair, but Winnie, with the speed and force of a jammer—she's a Roller Derby Hall of Fame inductee, you know—sent that poor deliveryman flying."

Winnie grabbed Kathryn's glass, which was about to spill, and both women were lost in near-delirious hysterics. Was I in a remake of *Arsenic and Old Lace*, but with Mortimer Brewster's eccentric aunts played by a fading swan and a roller derby queen? Had they slipped a little arsenic into my prosecco, and might they ultimately cart my limp body off in the wheelchair and bury me in their basement? But Luca's tail wagged, and I place a lot of faith in a dog's good instincts, so I figured I was safe.

Their laughter finally subsided. Winnie handed Kathryn her drink, and Kathryn said: "Probably Winnie's greatest pet peeve is when a parent gives a toddler an iPad or cell phone to stop him from fussing, like a high-tech pacifier. Such things don't bother me. I figure it's all part of evolution."

"Devolution is more like it," Winnie muttered.

"See what I mean, Haber? If it were up to Winnie, we'd all sit around a fire grunting."

"I'm afraid I agree with Winnie," I said. "Well, not about grunting."

"Winnie, you may have met your soul mate," Kathryn said.

Winnie definitely rolled her eyes this time, and another twenty minutes or so passed with light chatter, mostly between Kathryn and me. I mentioned the Metropolitan exhibits I was reading about when she first asked me about Luca, and she mentioned that she was once a docent at the Metropolitan. "Until…," and Kathryn pointed at the wheelchair. The near-empty flute slipped from her fingers, and she pressed her palms against the blanket as if to steady herself.

Before I could ask if she was all right, Winnie scooped Kathryn up and lowered her into the wheelchair.

"I told you to rest today," Winnie snapped.

Kathryn brushed her trembling fingers against her brow. "I'm fine. Stop making a fuss. Haber will regret having joined us."

I lifted the crystal flute from the blanket, but Winnie grabbed it out of my hand and patted the small wet spot with a napkin.

"A little prosecco never hurt anything. It will dry," Kathryn said, sounding unsure.

Winnie scraped the remaining cheese and fruit back into the Tupperware.

"There's no need to leave. Haber hasn't finished

eating." But Winnie ignored Kathryn's comments and packed everything up. I barely had time to stand before she pulled the blanket out from under me and folded it. Her expression and mannerisms warned me not to interfere, but I couldn't just leave without offering some assistance. Luca stood next to Kathryn's chair and rested his head on her lap. She didn't seem to notice him.

"At least let me carry the basket," I said.

For the first time, Winnie made direct eye contact with me, and she shoved the basket into my stomach. Given the circumstances, I didn't argue. Luca and I just followed her as she pushed Kathryn's chair along the grass, and then onto the concrete path. We were out of the park in no time, and Winnie took a cell phone from her breast pocket, and then called someone and explained our location.

I asked Kathryn if she was feeling better, and sensed Winnie bristling as if the mere sound of my voice angered her. I was tempted to tell her that the damn picnic wasn't my idea, but I held my tongue.

"I'm fine," Kathryn said. "Winnie's just an old mother hen. I had one of my nasty treatments yesterday, and…."

"And you should have rested today," Winnie snapped again.

"See what I mean," Kathryn said. Her voice had lost its dazzle, and her hands sat trembling in her lap.

A black Escalade parked in front of us, and a young man in a crisp, white shirt and black slacks rushed from the car and opened the rear passenger door. Again Winnie lowered herself over Kathryn, and Kathryn clasped her fingers behind Winnie's neck. Winnie held Kathryn's back and slowly pivoted toward the Escalade's rear bench-seat. The young man folded the wheelchair and carried it to the rear of the car while Winnie fastened Kathryn's seatbelt, closed Kathryn's door, and grabbed the basket from my hand, spun round, and left me standing there as if nothing had changed since our altercation earlier under the spindly locust tree; however, in the brief moment before she turned away from me, I noticed that Winnie's eyes welled with tears. What could I say?

I didn't know the specifics of Kathryn's condition, but it appeared serious, possibly fatal, and I felt sorry for her. I also felt sorry for Winnie. Whatever Kathryn and Winnie's relationship, I sensed that losing Kathryn would be a tremendous blow for Winnie.

Kathryn lowered the tinted window. She struggled to give her voice a little flair. "Thank you for a lovely afternoon, Haber."

I told Kathryn that I was sorry—a trite comment, but it was true.

"No need to be sorry, Haber. I had a wonderful time," Kathryn said wistfully, as if she were recalling much more than a picnic, and then she held out her small, trembling fist. "Someday, a gift for your Ava. She was wonderful in The Barefoot Contessa."

I don't know if Kathryn was trying to be witty or if, given her state, she had somehow confused my grand-daughter with The Barefoot Contessa's Ava Gardner, but as the Escalade pulled away, she opened her hand and her onyx and diamond cocktail ring spilled into my palm. I almost dropped it, and by the time I realized what had taken place and looked up, the Escalade had vanished.

The next day and every day until I left for home, I alternated walks in Carl Schurz Park with walks in Central Park, hoping to cross paths with Kathryn and Winnie, and to return the ring, but some things are just not meant to be.

My family returned on the following Saturday. Ava sat on my lap during dinner. She was exhausted and barely touched her food. I inhaled the scent of sun and beach, admired the summer gold that had highlighted her brown curls, and was reminded of Winnie's toast, *To Haber's son, son-in-law, and grandchild.* Soon Ava dozed against my shoulder, and I told Aaron and Darius about the picnic and about having met Winnie earlier while walking my dogs. I also showed them the ring and told them that Kathryn wanted it to go to Ava.

I shrugged my shoulders, and said: "Maybe her chemo or whatever treatment she was going through hindered her judgment. She was quite the character with all her talk of famed authors and painters and actors. But she was also lovely. A refreshing throwback to a more cordial time."

"And apparently very generous," Aaron said.

"From your description of the two women," Darius said, "I think Ava has more in common with Winnie than Kathryn. Not sure she'll be into cocktail rings, but I bet she'll love the roller derby."

"Then you can wear the ring," Aaron said to Darius, and the three of us laughed.

I was grateful to have my family home and safe. Kathryn had reminded me of life's fragility.

The following morning, I walked the dogs along Central Park Lake. Except for slight wakes that trailed a mother duck and her brood, the lake was still and mirrored the blue sky and white clouds. I unfolded my newspaper on a bench and sat. Luca lay at my feet. Gertrude snapped at bees, and I inhaled the aroma of the strong coffee from my thermos. An egret rose from a clump of reeds and a lone swan glided near where I sat. The morning sun illuminated its blue-white feathers, like delicate ribbons of iridescent cellophane.

Gertrude didn't share my admiration for the lovely swan, and she pulled at her lead and barked. The swan tilted its head and focused one onyx eye on Gertrude. Of course I thought of Kathryn, Winnie, and of Kathryn's gift. Maybe Kathryn had been one of Truman Capote's swans after all, or maybe she had read the same article about him that I had read, and had fashioned her own Gilded Age at dinner parties where her blond English lab posed for caviar, and later at picnics with the odd opera singer, gay tour guide reminding her of Truman, and a curmudgeon arborist.

Gertrude cowered behind my legs, Luca sniffed at the air. I hoped that Aaron was correct. He believed that Kathryn's gift was intentional, and that it comforted her to know that years from now, when I'd give Ava the ring, I would also speak of the picnic.

The swan lingered for a few moments, but then turned and drifted away from us.

Grave Companions

On damp rainy days when umbrellas and hurried steps spoke of solitary lives, Sal found solace at the diner beneath the El. He sat in a booth on a cracked vinyl bench, his forearms pressed against a chipped Formica table, most of its yellow faded to white, and he contemplated patrons shaking loneliness from their coats and hats and sometimes from their hair, making luminous haloes like in the pictures of saints on his bedroom dresser, where Tillie once lit tall slender vigil candles. Customers wearing glasses removed them and wiped beads of water from their lenses while others dabbed their eyes with paper napkins.

Sometimes Sal perched on a stool at the counter among strangers reading newspapers and drinking coffee, and he remembered holiday meals when his extended family and friends crowded around the dining room table made longer with four leaves, and Tillie was the pulse of the feast, not just because she was in constant motion replenishing empty plates, but because with great animation she also fed them stories and laughter. Sal hungered for those stories and for that laughter and for Tillie. Today would have been their sixtieth wedding anniversary.

Sal looked beyond his quivering mug of hot coffee and spotted a woman sitting at a table for two in the front window where the name Scarpentonio's was stenciled in reverse. It was one thing to sit alone in a booth or at a counter, but quite another to sit alone at a table for two where the sole chair facing you is pointless. Sal told himself it was the steam from his coffee that moistened his eyes. She smiled at him, not Tillie's smile that once had made him real, but a warm smile nonetheless. Years ago, Sal would have blushed, but at his age a young woman's smile meant only a smile so he managed a thin curve of his lips in response, then looked down at his plate of eggs and home fries.

The diner smelled of damp raincoats, drenched umbrellas, coffee and bacon, hot grease from the grill, and of the hot layers of paint that bubbled and peeled away from old radiators like crumbling memories. And he pushed the eggs from one side of his plate to the other, then turned down his hearing aid because the noise of china and silverware overwhelmed conversations, and he wasn't really interested anyway.

His cup rattled and though he couldn't hear the train

he knew it had just left the station. The young woman with the warm smile was no longer sitting at her table for two, and he imagined her riding the departed train as it rattled past shaded windows in apartments above shabby storefronts, and then descended underground where it's too risky to give away smiles. Sal didn't ride the subway anymore or buses or even drive his car but a few blocks.

He drank the last bit of coffee, and then stared into the empty mug's spidery veins.

"More coffee, Pops?"

He turned up his hearing aid but lowered his eyes away from the lettering UNDER CONSTRUCTION stretched across the waitress's pregnant belly. His brow creased and his lips disappeared in a frown. "No, thank you, I have to say good-bye." The waitress dropped the check next to his left hand where a gold band girdled his gnarly ring finger, and she moved on without taking the time to understand.

Under the cavernous iron, wood, and cement of the El, rainwater dripped as if from a thousand stalactites, and Sal opened his black umbrella and shuffled across the avenue and beyond the El, where droplets turned to drizzle; he was cautious not to slip in the puddles of oily rain mixed with florets from Norway maples, and not to trip over broken concrete, where the sidewalk had yielded to tree roots and winter ice. He passed brick and stucco and vinyl-sided houses, one-family or two-family, with wrought-iron fences and scrolled grates on basement and first-floor windows, and BEWARE OF DOG signs even where no dogs lived. Windows were decorated with cardboard cutouts of Easter bunnies and crosses with white lilies and colorful eggs, while in small front gardens, fenced with brick crowned by wrought-iron trim, daffodils and tulips bowed before concrete Marys.

Umbrellas rushed past him, their bearers on their way to catch the train. Across the street, one umbrella moved as slowly as Sal's, and beneath it an old woman, dressed in black, hobbled along while pulling a cart filled with yesterday's news.

A private ambulance idled in front of Paolo's house, and Sal, though pleased that he'd made it in time, felt distraught by its sight and its implication; he didn't notice Angie sitting in her son's car. Before Paolo's stroke, Sal often visited and usually overstayed his welcome, but they felt sorry for him, and Angie always cooked more than enough.

Once Sal no longer drove except for a few blocks, Paolo would drive him to Saint John's Cemetery to visit Tillie's grave. Sometimes Angie joined them, and on their way home they'd stop for coffee at Dunkin' Donuts. Occasionally Angie packed a lunch, and after the cemetery they parked at a favorite spot, where they watched boats out on the bay, and planes leaving and arriving at LaGuardia Airport and trains passing in the distance, and they spoke about the past and finished each other's sentences the way friends with a long history often do.

After Paolo's stroke, Sal visited them only once. He told himself that trying to hold a conversation with Paolo frustrated his old friend. The stroke had taken Paolo's speech and left him with only a few nonsense words like "nippy" and "fenzo." Sal spoke with Angie by phone every Sunday.

Angie lowered her window and called to Sal through the drizzle. He couldn't hear her above the sound of raindrops tapping on his umbrella and cars splashing by, but he noticed Angie waving and approached the car.

"They're inside putting Paolo on a stretcher." Angie brought a tissue to her aquiline nose. "My son paid for a private ambulance. He thought his father would be more comfortable." She ran her thumb along the back of her wedding band. "I don't know."

Sal leaned closer to the car and held the umbrella over the open window to shield Angie. "Young people have their own ideas. This is good, Angie. You have a good son."

As if conflicted, she nodded her head but shrugged her shoulders. "It's too much for my son to keep driving down here. He's got his own family to worry about. I'm not so good about paying bills and getting things fixed. Paolo took care of all that." Again she shrugged, but also extended her hands, palms up like the garden Madonnas Sal had passed along the way. "I guess we'll sell the house, but I feel bad for the tenants. They've been good to us."

"One thing at a time, Angie." Sal wished he had offered to help Angie with bills and day-to-day maintenance, but Paolo would have disapproved. Friends, no matter how close, aren't family.

Angie pointed to the front of the two-family brick building where sixty-three years ago she had moved in as a bride. A huge man, his back arched over a stretcher, backed out of the front door and lumbered down the brick steps. Paolo's right arm shielded his eyes, and a second smaller man supported the end of the stretcher beneath Paolo's head. Behind them, Paolo's son locked the deadbolts and security doors, then followed the procession to where the attendants set his father's stretcher onto a gurney. The son opened an umbrella over his father, and Sal remembered a much younger Paolo, with arms that could lift a case of olive oil and swing it onto one of his broad shoulders as if it were a down-filled pillow. When they were boys, long before Sal took over his father's bakery and Paolo his father's grocery, Sal both admired and envied his friend's strength and his prowess at baseball. Across the street from where the ambulance now waited there was once an open field and Sal and Paolo and a band of first-generation American boys played baseball in the trampled-down weeds on humid summer evenings, until the moon and fireflies were the only light, and hungry mosquitoes feasted on the boys' bare legs. Sal recalled the crack of the bat against the ball and the smell of low tide wafting in from Howard Beach as he watched his old friend jiggle across the broken sidewalk. He left Angie to her tears and approached the back of the ambulance, where the two attendants were about to lift the gurney, collapse its legs, and then roll the gurney into the ambulamnce. Paolo's son motioned for them to wait.

"Hello, Mr. Beltrani," he said, reaching for Sal's hand. Their umbrellas formed a black canopy over Paolo, and Paolo lowered his arm away from his face and clasped the hem of his friend's jacket. The attendants were wet and impatient. "I'm sorry, but we have to go, Mr. Beltrani," Paolo's son apologized. "We have a long drive ahead of us."

"Of course. I understand," Sal said, and leaned closer to his friend. "Don't make your son crazy." And he thought to kiss Paolo's forehead, but remembered doing the same to Tillie before the undertaker closed her casket and it felt too foreboding. Instead, he squeezed his friend's free hand.

Paolo released Sal's jacket and slowly waved the tips

of his fingers, and as the attendants lifted the gurney into the ambulance, he glanced back and, the way old couples mirror each other, he made the same shoulder and hand motions that Angie had made only a few moments earlier, and then he stretched his arm back over his eyes and his sleeve absorbed his tears.

"May I drive you home, Mr. Beltrani?" Paolo's son asked. He pulled a handkerchief from his pocket.

"No, thank you," Sal answered. "My car is parked on the avenue. I walked here from Scarpentonio's." They embraced, then parted.

Sal was unable to see if Angie waved through the curtains of drizzle, but he waved back nonetheless. The ambulance pulled away from the curb and the car followed. In the finality of the moment, Sal thought of Tillie and was reminded that since Paolo's stroke, he hadn't visited her grave, and the two months that had passed felt like forever—in the thirteen years since his wife's death, until he stopped driving his car but a few blocks, he had visited his wife's grave every day. There was his hospital stay for prostate surgery and the occasional holidays that were spent with his daughters, but such times were the exceptions.

Tillie had died when Sal still owned and operated his bakery, and everyday at lunchtime, he bought a sandwich and cream soda at Paolo's store, then drove to the cemetery. Next to Tillie's gravestone, he unfolded a small red camp seat that he kept in the back of his delivery truck, and he ate his lunch. If no one was around he talked to Tillie. Over the years he befriended a few regulars—mostly Italian old-timers—who visited the cemetery on weekends or for holidays and special occasions. They'd nod to each other, exchange a few words, and then go about their business of caring for the loved ones' graves and whispering prayers. Sal's truck with **BELTRANI'S BAKERY** stenciled across its side panels became as much a fixture at Saint John's Cemetery as the gravestones and mausoleums. On cold or rainy or snowy days, it provided shelter for Sal while he ate his sandwich, drank his soda, and talked to Tillie. More than a few of the regulars felt a tinge of regret when Sal replaced his truck with a Buick (after he sold his bakery)—just another reminder of loss, like a mound of freshly disturbed soil or a name added to a gravestone.

With Paolo and Angie went any hope of visiting Tillie's grave, which felt the same as no longer being able to visit Tillie. As he stood beneath the solitude of his umbrella and recalled that today would have been their anniversary, the loss felt unbearable, reminiscent of the grief he'd suffered almost thirteen years earlier on the day he stopped home for lunch to surprise Tillie with fresh warm Easter bread and a pot of hyacinths. His hands were full, so he pushed open the kitchen door with his hip, careful not to crack the pastel-colored hardboiled eggs peeking out from the warm golden braid of bread, or to crush the grape-smelling flowers. Tillie would have placed the flowers at the center of the kitchen table, then made espresso while Sal sliced the bread, and the aroma in the kitchen would be strong and sweet. They'd sit at the table and sip the espresso from demitasse cups that they had bought years ago in a little shop on Mulberry Street and spread whipped butter on chunks of warm bread and Tillie would begin, "This reminds me of the time we…." Something about the moment would have spurred one of Tillie's stories and Sal would smile and nod and he'd add a detail or two, and their reminiscing would become a dance of words and nods and laughter, and their rapport would spark more intimate feelings and they'd move from the kitchen to the bedroom.

But instead, when Sal entered the house, there was no sound of humming, or of Tillie's stockings rubbing against her skirt as she rushed about the rooms, and when he called out her name there was no answer. Unwashed breakfast dishes sat next to the sink and Tillie, in a cream-colored slip trimmed with lace, her hose balled up in her right hand, lay across her unmade bed. Sal stood at the bedroom door, holding out the Easter bread and hyacinths as if expecting his wife to rise and take her gifts from out of his hands.

You didn't say good-bye, Tillie, Sal thought as he watched the ambulance turn the corner onto the avenue under the El. No siren, no need, Tillie was gone. But then he remembered that it was Paolo, not Tillie, in the ambulance. Her silent ambulance had left thirteen years ago, a long time for Sal to wake up each morning regretting that he was still here.

———

Red lights provided respite, and he took deep breaths and gave himself pep talks and when the light turned green, slowly he raised his right foot from the brake and eased on the gas, anxious for the relief of another red light. Street names, stop signs, traffic, pedestrians, and kids on bicycles vied for Sal's attention. "Turn left on Woodhaven... watch out for that little boy... don't get too close to the bus." He spoke his actions aloud as he did when he turned off the coffeemaker on the kitchen counter or took his medications, as if reminding a child to complete his chores.

Three days had passed since he said goodbye to Paolo and Angie, and all he had thought about was going to the cemetery one last time, to tell Tillie he could no longer visit her. He considered calling one of his daughters to drive him, but they lived in Manhattan and whichever daughter agreed would first have to pick up her car at the garage, and then drive to Queens, and there'd probably be a lot of traffic. He quickly dismissed the idea. His daughters were slighter versions of their mother in appearance and in other ways, as if calorie-counting depleted them not only physically but also emotionally. They lacked their mother's generosity. Tillie was always the first to show up and the last to leave, offering food and laughter and tears and stories as if she were a human cornucopia; her daughters mostly offered excuses and apologies. Sorry, but I have a meeting, or my husband is working late, or the kids have a game, or I forgot but we already made plans. Sal loved and was proud of his daughters, and he tried not to blame them for not being their mother, but he knew not to depend upon them.

He drove beyond his imagined limits for the first time in almost two years, crawling in the far right lane of an eight-lane boulevard—four lanes traveling east and four lanes west. As a boy, Sal had biked the eastern route to the beaches, when this concrete boulevard was a gravel road that meandered through acres of marsh, where ibises, ospreys, herons, and egrets enjoyed the vast wetlands. He had seen the first two-lanes paved and every subsequent expansion since, just as he had seen wooden sidewalks become concrete and gas streetlights become electric and open land become rows of houses, stores, schools, churches, synagogues, and more recently a mosque, on a grid of streets intersecting avenues. The grid had been imprinted on his brain and revised multiple times and each time his brain rewired and accommodated, but as he drove west on Woodhaven Boulevard to Saint John's Cemetery, the once-familiar street names and landmarks seemed strange. Like the gravel roads he had biked as a boy, his thoughts meandered through the marshes of his memories. "Are you sure?" he asked himself aloud. "This doesn't seem quite right."

In all, Saint John's was about five miles from his house, and he had already driven halfway there when a Camaro peeled out around Sal's Buick and startled him. Sal glanced to his left, but within the blur of red and chrome he could barely make out the young driver and the driver's extended middle finger, before the Camaro swerved in front of him, and Sal, summoning some forgotten reserve of energy, jerked his steering wheel to the right and slammed on the brakes, just missing a parked taxi cab. He shook so violently that he was barely able to turn the key in the ignition. His head sank back into the headrest and his eyes closed. Again, he was startled, but this time by someone rapping on his car window. It was the cabbie whose car he had almost sideswiped, and Sal attempted to lower his window, forgetting that he had turned off the ignition.

"Open your door," the cabdriver yelled and Sal obeyed.

"Are you okay?"

"Yes, I think so," Sal answered, but his body continued to tremble and he was beginning to sweat.

"I saw that son of a bitch cut you off. Thought you were gonna slam right into me, but you didn't—no thanks to the jerk in the Camaro. You got pretty good reflexes for an old guy…. Are you sure you're okay? You don't look so good. Maybe I should call an ambulance."

Sal noticed the cabdriver pull a cell phone from his jacket. "No, no, I'll be fine. Just let me step out of the car and get some air." The last thing he wanted was to wind up in an emergency room. If he was going to die, let it happen near Tillie rather than in a hospital. The cabdriver's strong grip as he helped Sal out of his car made Sal feel frail and incompetent and reminded him of visiting Paolo after the stroke and how Paolo had cried. Sal feared that he might do the same in front of this stranger.

He leaned against his car, feeling small in the shadow of the cabdriver, who was as huge as the attendant that had helped carry Paolo's stretcher down the steps from his house.

"I'm feeling better already, and I'm glad it stopped raining." But from the cabbie's baffled expression—an expression that Sal often noticed lately—he knew that he had misspoke. He glanced at the dry pavement. "Guess I'm still a little shaky, but I'll be okay…. Really."

The cabdriver stroked his chin and shook his head as if unsure of Sal's assessment. "Think you can stay here alone for a minute? I'm gonna run in that store and get you something to drink."

"Yes, but there's no need for…." Before Sal could finish protesting the cabdriver disappeared into a small deli. The front window was papered with faded handmade signs advertising sandwich specials, bagels, and knish. "Tillie likes knish," Sal whispered. And he remembered all their times at Nathan's in Coney Island. After hours of amusement park rides and games, Sal would carry a tray piled high with hotdogs and French-fries and a knish for Tillie—sometimes with his daughters hanging on either side of him—back to where Tillie sat against a backdrop of lime-green walls, punctured with a row of porthole windows. She looked beautiful to Sal, like the feasts she prepared—colorful and bounteous. Her shiny hair was blacker than her large eyes and her full lips were redder than the blush of her cheeks, and her polka-dot sundress barely contained her ample breasts.

Still leaning against his car and staring at the rush of traffic, he realized that it wasn't only Tillie that he missed, but he missed being the one to carry the tray. He missed who he was with Tillie and who they were when the girls were young, and he also missed yeast and eggs and flour and never skimping on ingredients or on the time that it took to bake perfect breads for loyal customers. And he missed a way of living that had to do with priorities and being thorough and being there when you should be there and knowing that for family and friends you should always be there, and then it had to do with visiting his wife's grave, even though his daughters told him that Mama's not really there, which was just another excuse for not doing what you should. Then he thought of Paolo and of visiting him only once after his stroke, and Sal felt ashamed and wondered if his daughters took after him more than they did after their mother.

And he also wondered if hyacinths were in bloom beneath the name Filomena (Tillie) Beltrani, carved in pink granite. Last fall, Paolo had handed him each hyacinth bulb, one at a time, while Sal knelt on one knee and carefully planted the bulbs in the soil before Tillie's gravestone, as carefully as folding eggs into flour. With one gnarled hand pressed against the cool granite and with Paolo's support, he was able to slowly get back on his feet again. He regretted that Paolo and Angie would never see the hyacinths in bloom or smell their grape fragrance, and most likely neither would he, and he felt old and foolish for having tried to drive to the cemetery.

Then it dawned on him that the cabdriver could drive him the rest of the way to Tillie's grave. In fact, this could become routine—maybe not every day, but once a week. Why hadn't he thought of this before? Cabdrivers drive old folks to church and to supermarkets all the time. Why not to cemeteries? When you outlive your peers, you have little choice but to depend on strangers. They might stop at Dunkin' Donuts or where he and Angie and Paolo used to park by the bay. Then he recalled the cabdriver helping him out of the car and the expression on the cabdriver's face when he misspoke about the rain and he hated what he had become, and he wanted the cabdriver to know that he wasn't always like this. *Just ask Tillie*, he thought.

He leaned against his car, tilted his face up toward the sun, and closed his eyes. The hyacinths were in full bloom, deep, dense clusters of purple bells and he inhaled their sweet, grape perfume.

"Water?" the cabdriver said.

Sal opened his eyes, and the cabdriver handed him a bottle of water. "My name is Gabe."

Sal shook the cabdriver's strong hand and took a sip of water.

Fragile Moments

They sat in comfortable swivel chairs while the Zephyr meandered through a narrow canyon, and Paul leaned forward, craned his neck, and looked out of the glass dome that arched above the upper deck of the observation car. "Lovely," he said to no one in particular, but one of those androgynous girls with sundry piercings glanced up from her cell phone and followed his gaze to where the canyon's red ridge traversed the turquoise sky.

"I guess so," she said. Paul shifted his eyes away from the two hoops through her bottom lip and the fullness of her tummy.

Another baby having a baby, he thought and made an effort to chat. She mentioned that she was in coach and returned to texting. Maybe their age difference made her uneasy or maybe communicating with thumbs superseded speaking. Her thin flowered notebook slipped unnoticed from her seat into Paul's open satchel. She left without comment or notebook.

That night, cold air blew through window ledges and ceiling vents, and the unnatural glow from laptops, tablets, and cellphones gave passengers an eerie pallor—zombie correspondents with feverish fingers and thumbs. Paul grasped the overhead luggage rack to steady himself against the train's rocking. *Trains speed up at night*, he reminded himself as he stumbled over a stray foot, which retracted like a startled snail.

Finally he spied her sitting alone, behind a dexterous zombie, simultaneously negotiating a laptop, cell phone, and iPod. Her tummy betrayed her, and Paul gently laid the thin flowered notebook on her lap. She looked up. The sheen below her eyes suggested tears.

"I'm sorry," Paul said. "It must have gotten mixed in with my books."

She curled her brow. "What?"

"You sat next to me for a bit, so I assumed the notebook was yours. I didn't look inside." A fib. When Paul came upon the notebook, he opened it, thinking that he had mistakenly taken it from his daughter's apartment. He found a taped photograph inside its cover and immediately recognized the girl with her cheek pressed against a boy's—both so young and beautiful, the way that young people are always beautiful. Paul turned one page, and then another, until he'd read all of the girl's poetry—unpolished and verbose, but also sensual and morose. He reread each poem before he closed the book, smiling at how some things never change. Once, he also believed that one might die from a broken heart, but now he knew better.

"I must have dropped it," the girl said. "Thank you." She pressed her fingers against the notebook as if searching for its pulse and wiped her eyes with the palm of her free hand.

"Are you alright?" Paul asked.

"I'm good," she said. Paul smiled, nodded, and then turned to find his way back to the sleeper cars.

Paul had once traveled a lot by train before he discovered that Valium and a stiff drink made bearable being sealed in a cramped projectile, miles above the earth. But bearable never became enjoyable, and for nostalgia's sake he had looked forward to this long overdue cross-country train trip. He flew from New York to California, visited with his daughter and her wife in San Francisco, and then boarded the Zephyr out of Emeryville to return east. He offered the usual excuse when his daughter asked him if he'd someday leave the long winters and overcast skies of Central New York and move to California. "Who would teach my students that there's more to music than pop culture?" he said. Paul had never been a fan of California. He blamed *The Graduate* and its iconic *plastics* scene for souring him against the Golden State.

Paul rocked to the train's motion in his roomette's narrow berth and remembered past train trips, especially the one he took from Toronto to Vancouver at least fifty years ago. Back then he slept in a curtained berth, reminiscent of the ones in the Marilyn Monroe movie *Some Like It Hot*. During the day, the upper berth folded back against the wall, and the lower berth transformed into bench seats. A girl from Japan—barely twenty— had sat across the aisle from Paul. She was traveling with her American cousin, first across the United States from California to New York, where they then took a bus to Toronto and boarded the train to Vancouver. From Vancouver, she planned to fly back to Japan.

On the first day of their journey they exchanged polite chitchat, but that night, when Paul climbed down in the dark from his upper berth to find his way to the lavatory, light shone between the slightly askew curtains across the aisle. He lingered in the dark, occasionally staring at his fingernails and the callus on his left index finger, and then glancing up through the parted curtains. The Japanese girl sat behind the curtains with her legs crossed. She may have been reading, or meditating, or waiting for Paul. Upon his return from the lavatory, the curtains hung more askew. The following morning at breakfast, he learned that her name was Misaki.

When they arrived in Jasper, Paul, Misaki, and her

cousin disembarked, rented a car, and toured the Canadian Rockies. The trio filled the long days with hiking and whitewater rafting, Paul acquired a taste for nigiri sushi and sashimi, and in the brief twilight hours, Paul and Misaki fed each other's carnal appetites. To the lull of the train's ostinato, Paul remembered Misaki, and other lovers—girls with long hair and embroidered gauze dresses, or psychedelic T-shirts and cut-off jeans, and a boy resembling Jimi Hendrix whom Paul had met at Woodstock. Paul also thought of his wife and their thirty-year marriage, cut too short by a ruptured aneurysm and of the child they lost to brain cancer, and he wanted to tell the girl with the pierced lip that for better or worse people rarely die from broken hearts. Paul hoped that she heard the train whisper: "It will be all right…it will be all right…"

The next morning in the dining car, when breakfast was almost over, Paul lifted his cup of coffee and said to one of the dining car servers, "When I last rode on a train, the dishes were china, not plastic."

The server, who was at least Paul's age, maybe older, smiled—his face was a relief of dark wrinkles. "Progress? Or an excuse to get rid of dishwashers," he said. "So, what can I get you? Last call."

Paul checked off oatmeal with brown sugar and raisins on his menu. They exchanged thank-yous, and Paul looked out the window. He preferred looking up into clouds rather than down onto them. A family of four sat at the table before his; he overheard the younger of the two children call one of the men Daddy and the other Papa, and Paul thought of his daughter, and regretted that he and his wife had never taken her on a train trip.

The server returned with a plastic bowl of steaming oatmeal and several small cups—raisins, brown sugar, and extra milk. Paul glanced at his nametag. "Thank you, Cedric," he said. "I guess you've seen a lot of railroad changes over the years."

Cedric grinned. "I've seen a lot of everything. Some of those things aren't polite to talk about over breakfast."

Paul introduced himself and extended his hand. Cedric returned the courtesy.

"Well, Paul, it's a pleasure to meet you, but this is more of a good-bye shake than hello—this being my last trip. Once we arrive in Chicago, I'm done—retired I mean."

"Good for you. I keep meaning to retire. One of these days, I'll get around to it."

The girl with the pierced lip entered the dining car, and Cedric whispered to Paul, "Breakfast is over, but it looks like that little girl is eating for two." After he directed the girl to the empty seat across from Paul and handed her a menu, Cedric joined his coworker in cleaning off and resetting tables for lunch.

"Good morning," Paul said. The girl stared at him through puffy eyes. Her short hair was spiked—whether from sleep or intentionally—similar to how she had worn it yesterday.

"Good morning," she mumbled then lowered her eyes to her menu.

"The oatmeal is good."

"I hate oatmeal," she said.

"Ahh, you're like my daughter." Paul chuckled.

The view of Utah was striking—more red against a turquoise sky, stone arches washed with sunlight, and asymmetrical blocks precariously stacked as if by a giant toddler—and Paul wondered if he should head to the observation car or make one last attempt at conversation. The girl made red pencil slashes on the menu, and he recalled the fine lines of blood on his daughter's arm— barely thirteen when she started cutting.

"I don't mean to intrude, but you seemed sad last night when I returned your book. I'm not a lecher, just a dad, old enough to be your grandfather. Are you really all right?"

She looked up. Her eyes were warm and large, and he smiled at her. "My name is Paul, or you can call me Mr. Berg if that makes you more comfortable."

"I'm Abby."

"Glad to meet you, Abby," Paul said.

After breakfast, Paul leaned against a post in the observation car; all of the seats were taken. The Zephyr snaked its way high into the Rockies, in and out of tunnels, while each flash of sunlight captured another spectacular image of barren mountain summits or lush valleys. Several passengers called out to look left, where above the tunnel's black arch a bachelor herd of bighorn sheep steadied their massive bodies along the craggy cliff face. Some flaunted their splendid horns and glanced indifferently at the tons of steel curving out from the mountainside beneath them.

Paul stared at the scene until the sheep were specks. He was distracted by thoughts of Abby and glad that he had lingered at breakfast. They'd made small talk— at first about favorite foods and movies and music. It turned out that Abby had an eclectic taste in music, and she knew a lot about what had been popular when Paul was young. He also learned that Abby was from Chicago, her mother was a dental hygienist, her father was in construction, and she had two younger siblings. Eventually her comments became more personal.

"Last September, I was supposed to start college," she said, "but I had a big fight with my parents. Instead of college, I left Chicago for California."

She didn't say what the fight had been about or if she had gone to California alone. Nor did she mention her pregnancy, and Paul didn't ask. Paul also discovered

Abby's pretty smile. Without the frown or tears, Abby was lovely and a bit puckish like a sprite or fairy.

When they finished breakfast and ran out of words, they parted. Nothing life-changing, but for the moments they shared Abby seemed happy, and Paul had learned to make the most of moments—one of the small wisdoms he acquired with age. Abby's falling-out with her parents reminded Paul of when his daughter dropped out of college and the argument that ensued between them, culminating with his daughter yelling "Fuck you," slamming the front door, and taking the next flight to San Francisco, not knowing that her mother would die from a ruptured aneurysm before there was time for amends. Paul had long ago forgiven his daughter, but he doubted that she forgave herself, and he had yet to forgive himself for not maintaining a cooler head.

That evening, Paul postponed dinner until the final call, when the Colorado sky was awash with pinks and lavenders. The sun dawdled atop the horizon flooding the dining car with light beams each time the eastbound Zephyr veered north or south. The car hummed with friendly conversation, reminiscent of a less hurried and more gracious era. Paul enjoyed his grilled tilapia despite the plastic dinnerware and, though he preferred drinking from glass stemware, his wine complemented the fish nicely.

His dinner companions included newlyweds who had just honeymooned in Frazier-Winter Park, Colorado, and a newly retired librarian whose father had once been a gate guard at MGM Studios. Their conversation was interrupted by the time-honored tradition of campers mooning the Zephyr from the banks of the Colorado River, and after some laughter, they resumed talk about Hollywood's Golden Age stars. The young couple's eyes glazed over when the librarian dropped names like Greer Garson or Lionel Barrymore, but sparkled when she mentioned having met Lucille Ball. Paul shared his knowledge of notable Hollywood composers like Max Stein and Franz Waxman, and the librarian nodded approvingly. By the time they finished dessert, only a dim backlight traced the horizon.

Cedric waited tables at the other end of the dining car, and as Paul left, he made a point of speaking to him. "Guess this is your swan-song dinner," Paul said.

Cedric leaned in close to Paul as if to whisper, "Glad to see that our little friend was smiling after you two finished breakfast this morning. I hate to see kids so down and out—especially her being in the family way."

"You're a good man, Cedric."

"By the way," Cedric said, "stop down about ten o'clock for some farewell cake."

The librarian followed Paul to the observation car where

they continued their conversation about film and film composers over another glass of wine. A writer and Tennessee Williams
enthusiast from New Orleans overheard them and joined in.
The writer and the librarian debated the acting merits of Elizabeth Taylor in *Cat on a Hot Tin Roof* versus Anna Magnani in
The Rose Tattoo, while Paul scanned the car for Abby.

It was a little after ten when Paul returned to the dining car. The tables were set for tomorrow's breakfast with
white tablecloths, white paper napkins, plastic settings
(four at each table), and carnations in narrow glass vases.
Cedric sat with two attendants.

"Come join us," Cedric called. "Hakeem, get my
friend a piece of cake. Paul, this is Tamika, and that big
guy slicing you some cake is Hakeem."

Paul slid in along the bench seat so Hakeem could sit
next to him, and he thanked him for the cake.

"Folks been coming and going all night, when they get
a break. Glad you could make it," Cedric said.

"This is the end of an era," Tamika said, then lifted a
napkin from the table and patted her eyes.

"So where's the cake?" Paul recognized the voice and
turned to see Chris, the attendant from his sleeper car.

"You know I'm not getting up again. Get your own
damn cake, man," Hakeem said.

"You're in room nine?" Chris said to Paul, and the
conversation flowed easily—a banter about past trips,

mishaps, and eccentric passengers. Some of the stories were racy, and Paul felt as if he were a student privy to teacher-room gossip. He thought of Misaki and wondered if attendants had once joked about them: *Did you catch that skinny, big-eared white boy with that pretty Asian girl? That won't last.*

"Here goes the preacher man," Chris shouted when Cedric began lecturing them on railroad history. Cedric had clearly told these stories many times.

"You kids don't know nothing unless Beyoncé sings it," Cedric said, and Paul was amused by Cedric referring to adults, probably in their thirties, as kids. "What do you do for a living?" Cedric asked Paul.

"I teach high school," Paul answered.

"There!" Cedric pounded his fist on the table. "He knows what I'm talking about!" Cedric was on a roll, and Paul wondered if he'd been drinking more than coffee.

"My great grandfather went from being a slave to getting a job as a Pullman porter. And my grandfather was a union organizer under A. Philip Randolph. But I'm the last railroad man in my family." Cedric looked at Paul. "Did you know that Thurgood Marshall was a descendent of a Pullman porter?"

"Don't go quizzing Paul," Tamika said. "I think Cedric makes up half this stuff."

Cedric rolled his eyes, and the other attendants laughed.

"I just know we got a lot of history in these trains. Some of it's good and some of it's not so good. If oil people had had their way, they would have gotten rid of trains long ago. We all know that ridership is up, but it don't put money in the man's pocket like oil does. At least we got Biden on our side. Be proud of Obama, but be grateful for Amtrak Joe."

By now Tamika, Hakeem, and Chris were waving their hands and laughing, and though Paul felt like the awkward, new kid on the block, he also felt privileged to share in Cedric's final night as an Amtrak employee.

One by one, Tamika, Hakeem, and then Chris returned to work, leaving Paul alone with Cedric. Lights flashed in the blackness outside the windows, and Cedric stared through the glass.

"It's been a long ride," he said. "These young folk don't get it. They're young. Guess they're not supposed to get it."

Paul and Cedric swapped stories about their children, and Cedric also included stories about his grandchildren. A few more attendants drifted in and out, and finally Paul excused himself and thanked Cedric for the invitation. "I'll wait until tomorrow to say good-bye," Paul said.

On the way back to his room, Paul passed Chris who was making up a bed in a roomette. "Quite a guy," Chris said. "We're gonna miss him."

Paul checked his cell phone. A text from his daughter: "we miss you already...come back soon...new condos for sale."

Tomorrow he'd call her. For now, he swayed to the train's rocking and thought of what Cedric had said about his own children: "One's a doctor, one's a social worker, and my youngest is in prison. Same parents, same neighborhood, but the street got my baby, and there was no getting him back."

Paul was grateful that his daughter was doing well—two master's degrees, a good job, a loving long-term relationship, and now she and her wife were considering parenthood. Regardless, he knew that some mistakes can't be undone. The heat of a moment could land someone in prison, like Cedric's youngest, or could forever be sealed as an angry farewell. Paul worried about Abby. *Do her parents know she's pregnant?*

The Zephyr's windows changed from morning fog to panoramas of Iowa's sun-bleached rolling plains, as Paul lay awake, considering the optimism a new morning offers.

He showered and dressed, grabbed a cup of coffee at the snack bar, exchanged good mornings with one of the attendants he had met last night, then headed up the narrow stairwell to the observation deck where a few passengers sat reading newspapers, hard copies or on laptops—occasionally they looked out over the prairies and farm fields.

Abby sat alone at the far end of the car. She was writing and Paul didn't want to intrude, but she noticed him and waved him over. She wore sweats, her hair needed washing, and the flowered notebook sat open on her lap.

Paul told Abby about the people he'd met last night at dinner and about Cedric's farewell gathering. Abby said that coach smelled ripe and that one of the toilets was out of order. She hadn't slept well.

"I was worried about today," Abby said.

Paul didn't respond. He remembered his daughter yelling, "You never listen!" So he waited quietly for Abby to say more.

"I wanted to have an abortion, but he said no."

Paul assumed that "he" was the boy in the picture— the picture taped to the inside of Abby's notebook.

"He said that abortion is a sin, that we'd get married. Two months later, he said he's not ready to be a father and that I should give the baby up for adoption." Abby's tears wet the pages of her poetry.

"I'm so sorry, Abby," was all he could think to say. They sat quietly, as the train rocked and Paul recalled a lullaby his wife used to sing to their daughter years ago.

Abby barely whispered, "They don't know."

"They?" Paul said.

"My parents. They don't know I'm pregnant. We've talked a few times on the phone, but they don't even know

I'm on this train. They don't know I'm coming home."

Paul's stomach tightened; he couldn't help but remember. If only *his* daughter had given him fair warning—rather than trumpeting, on the day before she was to return to college after Thanksgiving break, "By the way, I've dropped out and there's nothing you can do about it." Maybe Paul wouldn't have exploded. Maybe the years of struggling to keep his daughter afloat through her teenage bouts with depression and bulimia, cutting, alcohol and drug abuse wouldn't have suddenly felt like an unbearable weight, and he wouldn't have reminded her of every mistake she had ever made. Maybe his daughter wouldn't have yelled "Fuck you" and gone off to San Francisco, and maybe she and her mother would have had time together before the aneurysm separated them forever.

"Abby, please don't make your parents the enemy," Paul said. "Give them a chance. Call them, or call someone else who can tell them that you're coming home. Without some warning, the shock might make things worse.

Abby clutched her notebook. She got up and left, and Paul laced his fingers together and sighed.

Later, Paul picked at his lunch, and he was poor company for the others at his table. They chatted on about the eagles they had seen earlier when the Zephyr neared the Mississippi River, but Paul claimed to have been reading at the time, even though he hadn't been reading. In fact, he had seen the eagles. He just wasn't in the mood to talk about it.

After lunch, he spent the remainder of the trip in his room, packing and reading. He thought to call his daughter, but decided to wait until Chicago. His door was ajar, and Cedric poked his head into Paul's room. They wished each other well and promised to be in touch, maybe take an Amtrak trip together someday, but they knew they never would.

Before Cedric left, he handed Paul a folded sheet of paper. "This was taped to your door. Must be from an admirer." Cedric closed the door on his way out.

Paul unfolded the paper and recognized it from Abby's flowered notebook: *I'll call my parents.*

There was a two-hour layover in Chicago, before Paul's train would leave for New York. In Union Station's Great Hall, commuters shouted into cell phones and bumped past each other without apologizing or making eye contact. Paul found a seat on one of the oversize wooden benches.

He spotted Cedric with a middle-aged woman and two teenagers, probably Cedric's daughter and his grandchildren. Paul removed his phone from his jacket pocket, and again looked up, and this time he saw Abby. She was walking arm in arm with a woman, and a man carried Abby's backpack—his free arm draped across her shoulder.

Paul smiled and looked down at his daughter's contact information on his screen.

Emma's

Emma's latest guests were an unlikely couple, not because the man was white and the woman black, but because he looked like someone who just rolled out of a sleeping bag, and she resembled someone you'd find at a perfume counter on Madison Avenue.

They'd arrived late the night before, after Emma fell asleep. For late arrivals, Emma emailed her guests the combination to the front-door lock beforehand, and then left room keys in a sterling silver basket on the Chippendale butler's table in the front foyer.

"Good morning," she said. "I'm Emma Pierce. You must be the Levs."

He yawned and covered his mouth with his broad, calloused hand—nails chewed to the quick and cuticles cracked and raw. The woman glanced from his yawn to Emma's smile. "I'm sorry. We had a very late night. I'm Monique Daws. This is my brother-in-law Joe Lev."

Emma wondered why Joe was with a sister-in-law instead of a wife, but of course she didn't ask. "Hopefully everything went well," Emma said.

"Yes. I think so," Monique answered. "My nephew just took awhile to shake the anesthesia. He wasn't discharged from the hospital until after midnight."

"The kitchen closes soon, but if he's still asleep, we can keep his breakfast warm."

"Thank you, but he's already awake. I understand that you'll prepare a tray for us to take up to him?"

Joe sat with his cheek pressed against the heel of his hand and his eyes half closed, oblivious or at least indifferent to his sister-in-law taking charge.

"Sure, or I can have it sent to your room," Emma said. "Would the two of you also like breakfast?"

"I'll have coffee and the fruit cup. Joe, you should eat something."

"Just coffee," he mumbled.

"And your son?" Emma directed the question to Joe, but Monique answered: "Avi will have the pancakes with bacon. He didn't eat at all yesterday."

"I'll get your coffee and fruit cup while Libby prepares Avi's breakfast." Emma spoke Libby and Avi's names as if they had all been friends for years. Two other guests finished eating their breakfast, but since Joe didn't seem to be up for socializing, Emma chose to forego introductions.

After telling Libby to cook a full breakfast, including pancakes and bacon for tray service, Emma spooned blueberries and cubes of cantaloupe into crystal stemware, then lifted a pot of coffee from its burner and returned to the dining room where Joe and Monique, now the only guests in the dining room, spoke in muted voices. Emma felt as if she were intruding. She placed the fresh fruit cup on the table, poured their coffees, cleared the plates from the other table, and then returned to the kitchen where she wiped a black lacquer tray with a damp cloth and covered the tray with a white paper doily. She poked her head through the swinging doors into the dining room. This time Monique glanced her way.

"Avi's breakfast is almost ready," Emma said. "Would you like me to carry it up to your room or keep it warm?"

Joe answered without looking at Emma. "No, I'll take it when it's ready."

When she returned with the tray, Joe downed the last of his coffee. He was in need of a shave and (Emma thought) a haircut, but a dreamy luster lit his large brown eyes, as if he had just awoken. Emma imagined him saying, *Good morning. Did you sleep well?*

As he took the tray from her hands, his fingers brushed hers, but he didn't seem to notice. She listened to the scrape of Monique's high heels on the stairs as they headed up, mixed with Joe's more contemplative steps.

———

Emma sat at a mahogany desk in the alcove beyond the parlor. Portraits in ornate frames of someone's family—not Emma's—hung on the wall behind her. Again she heard the scrape of Monique's high heels, looked up from her computer, and smiled.

"I hope I'm not intruding."

"Not at all," Emma said. She recognized the fragrance of Monique's perfume, but couldn't recall its name. "Lovely earrings. I'm partial to silver. Goes with anything." Emma held up her hand to display her rings and a silver bracelet. "I bought these in a shop on Larch Street. Hopefully you'll find time to tour our little town."

"Unfortunately I'm leaving now. I have a meeting early tomorrow morning that I'm not able to postpone, and D.C. is a four-hour drive from here. But first, I'd like to ask you something."

Normally Emma would have interpreted a guest's mention of work as an invitation for small talk—*D.C.? An exciting city. Have you lived there long? Don't tell me you're in politics*—but given that Monique was in a hurry, Emma took her at her word and remained silent.

"Joe said that Dr. Austin had recommended your B&B, that many of her patients have stayed here."

Emma nodded. She pointed to a rosewood chair, upholstered with flowered tapestry. "Please, won't you sit?"

"Only for a minute. I have to get on the road, but I'm torn about leaving." Monique paused as if to gather her thoughts. "Since you're familiar with Dr. Austin's patients, I assume that you know why we're here."

"Dr. Austin, of course, doesn't share the particulars about her patients. That would be unethical. But yes, many of her patients have been my guests, and I assure you that your nephew is more than welcome. Whatever he needs, I will do my best to accommodate."

"I appreciate that." Again Monique seemed distracted. "You see this is very difficult. Maybe this is too much information, but as I said I couldn't postpone my meeting." She took a deep breath and picked at a pearl button on the sleeve of her blouse. "My brother passed away not quite two years ago." Monique's voice quivered.

"How terrible," Emma said. She slid a box of tissues toward Monique instinctively; but she was confused as to why Monique mentioned a brother.

"Thank you. And my parents were very much against Avi's surgery, and Joe's parents were not much better. Avi's only sixteen, you know."

Now Emma understood. Joe had been married to Monique's brother, not a sister, as Emma had assumed when Monique introduced him as her brother-in-law.

Monique dabbed at the corners of her eyes. She sighed, removed a wallet from her purse, slipped out her business card, and placed the card on the desk before Emma. "This has my cell number on it. Please call me if you sense any problems. Joe won't call. He doesn't like to impose."

Both women stood, and Emma followed Monique through the parlor to the front foyer, where she responded to Monique's hug with a curt pat on the back. She assured Monique that her brother-in-law and nephew would be fine.

After closing the front door, Emma remembered the mother and her teenager daughter who had stayed at the B&B the summer before. The mother confided in Emma that while still in kindergarten her daughter complained that God made a mistake, that she wasn't a boy. She was a girl.

A week passed before the teenager left her room at Emma's B&B and joined her mother in the dining area for breakfast. She was slender and quite lovely, like a model on the cover of *Seventeen*. Her dark brown hair was brushed back in a ponytail and she wore a flowered sundress. She also carried a post-op donut pillow that she placed on her chair before sitting. There was something emblematic about the pillow, and while watching the girl arrange herself atop it, Emma thought, *she's too young for such challenges and to make such choices*. Avi was the second teenage patient of Dr. Austin's to stay at Emma's B&B.

Also too young, Emma thought, but she knew first hand that life made no concessions for youth.

———

Being an adroit businesswoman who understood synergy, Emma considered antique shops, summer-stock theater, restaurants, and B&Bs to be the four pillars supporting the town's tourist economy. She promoted the local antique dealers, served on the board of directors for the summer-stock theater—where she swayed the more provincial members to extend the season through December, a boon not only for the theater but also for the town at large—and dined weekly at local restaurants, then wrote flattering reviews that she shared with her guests and with the other B&Bs. So it was no surprise that three years ago a prominent plastic surgeon, opening a new practice in the area, contacted Emma, a luminary among the town's business community. They met at a local restaurant for lunch, and as usual Emma arrived early. She added a drop of cream to her Earl Grey, wiped the already spotless teaspoon with a napkin, stirred her tea three times, and then patted the chignon at the nape of her neck—posing as if she expected paparazzi. Between sips of tea, she hummed and scanned the pages of Vogue, sweeping each page with her fingertips as if directing an invisible orchestra.

"Have you been waiting long?" A tall woman stood before Emma.

"I'm Dr. Austin. Please call me Dana. I recognized you from your website photos." Dana extended her hand as she took the seat across from Emma. "Thank you for meeting with me."

"My pleasure." After Emma released Dana's hand, she motioned to the empty tables and chairs. "As you can see, this is not exactly a bustling time of year."

Dana removed her coat and scarf and draped them over the back of her chair. She wore a black cowl-neck sweater, and her red hair fell soft to her shoulders. Her earrings sparkled as she pushed her hair away from her face. Emma had also searched online for information about this plastic surgeon, soon to open a practice less than a mile from Emma's B&B, and learned that not only did Dr. Austin specialize in sex reassignment surgery, but she had undergone such surgery herself some eight years ago, transitioning from male to female.

Given the town's businesses and tourists, Emma was no stranger to gay men and, to a lesser degree, lesbians. Surely she had also met transgender people, probably without realizing it. She studied Dr. Austin's features and movements for telltale hints of masculinity. *How small-minded of me,* she thought, then complimented Dana on her sweater.

"I think local businesses will benefit from my practice, especially B&Bs," Dana said. "I reached out to you since you seem to be well connected."

No nonsense. Right to the point, Emma thought. *Just like a man*. Then Emma chuckled to herself. *Actually, just like me*.

"Have you ladies decided?" The young waiter held the nub of a pencil to his pad.

"Matteo, this is Dr. Austin. She's the new kid in town. I know lunch will be delicious. That's why I recommended this restaurant." Emma didn't add that it was also one of the few restaurants open—January through March tourists were scarce.

"Welcome, Dr. Austin." Matteo extended his hand, smiled, and lowered his canopy of long eyelashes, which Emma had long coveted.

"We may need a few more minutes," Emma said.

"Sure, just wave when you're ready."

"Sweet boy," Emma said. "Now you were suggesting that B&Bs would benefit from your practice. How so?"

Dana explained that most of her surgeries were done through outpatient services. The hospital that she was affiliated with was five miles away, but she thought that her patients would prefer to stay in town, given the town's charm and its proximity to her new office. "After a few days, depending on the surgery, my patients are well enough to go out. Motels near the hospital are on a major thoroughfare, not a pleasant walking area. Recovering in a safe, comfortable, and nurturing environment is crucial. And, I believe, so is an aesthetically pleasing environment—like Emma's...at least from what I've seen from your website photographs."

As Dr. Austin had predicted, once her practice opened, Emma booked year-round, with even some spillover for the other B&Bs. Emma had developed an affinity for many of the guests that Dr. Austin referred to her. After their stay, she kept in touch through email or on Facebook, and some guests returned for vacations, often women who had lived for many years as men and sought out Emma's advice about all things feminine. She had a penchant for details and was a master at reinvention.

Eighteen years before meeting Dr. Austin, a motorcycle accident had left Emma a young widow, and a savvy lawyer had afforded her the means to reinvent herself from the daughter of an abusive mother, turned wife of an equally abusive husband, into an independent and successful entrepreneur. After receiving the insurance money from her husband's accident, she changed her name to Emma Pierce—Emma because she liked the sound of it and Pierce for Mildred Pierce, the Joan Crawford character in one of Emma's favorite Turner Classic films. Next, she bought a used Mercedes and drove it to no place in particular, until she came upon a quaint tourist town in Pennsylvania, bordering New Jersey, with a fixer-upper B&B for sale. Given her financial windfall, her keen eye, and the example of Turner Classics' audacious female characters, Emma turned the fixer-upper into a blue-ribbon B&B and called it Emma's.

Like the guests Dr. Austin referred to her, Emma was a survivor.

———

Behind the heavy wood door to her private suite—a comfortable sitting room, with an adjoining bedroom, and bathroom—Emma heard little of her guests' comings and goings. She thought to check on Joe and Avi, but she didn't. Joe struck her as reticent, and she didn't want to intrude. She saw him again the next morning, toward the end of breakfast.

"Am I too late?" He was more put together than yesterday: clean-shaven, his hair combed, and he wore tan slacks and a blue short-sleeve button-down shirt.

"Not at all," Emma said. "We serve breakfast until ten. You'll also want a tray for Avi? We have French toast and, of course, eggs, made however he would like them."

"He'll have the French toast, but I'll have fried eggs."

"Two?"

"Please." *Not only does he clean up well, but he can also be polite,* Emma thought.

"Coffee, juice, and a fruit cup?"

"Thank you. That would be great." Joe sat at a table next to the window, looking out on the gardens. Foxglove and coneflowers were in bloom—Emma grew them from seed.

"Are you an herbalist?" Joe said.

"No, why do you ask?" Emma said, a bit perplexed.

"Your flowers. Darnell used to dabble in that stuff. You know, like echinacea." Joe stared through the window-pane out onto the garden.

"Darnell?" Emma said, though, given her conversation with Monique, she assumed that she already knew who he was.

"Yes, my partner. I mean, he was my partner. He's passed away." Sunlight exaggerated the furrows a comb had left in Joe's thick, wet black hair.

"I'm sorry," Emma said.

Joe shrugged and smiled then turned his eyes from the garden to Emma.

"And you?" Emma said. "Are you also a gardener and an herbalist?" She traced the back of a chair with her fingertips.

"Me?" Joe broadened his smile until it engaged all of his features. "No, I'm a painter. Houses, not canvas. And an amateur musician."

Emma glanced at Joe's hands—no flecks of paint beneath the wisps of black hairs, just a simple gold wedding band.

"The calluses are from strumming my guitar," he said, turning his palms up for her to see.

Embarrassed, Emma turned her head away. "I'll give Libby your breakfast order," she said.

After telling Libby what to prepare, she turned to Libby's daughter. "Please bring the man wearing a blue Oxford shirt coffee, juice, and a fruit cup. I have bills to pay."

Joe wasn't that much younger than Emma. Maybe two or three years, at most five. She stood before her bedroom mirror, then removed her hairpins and wondered if she looked younger or older with her hair down.

Emma obsessed over her appearance the way she obsessed over place settings and curtains and bedspreads, but when she examined her reflection, Emma wasn't seeking her own approval. She wondered what Joe saw when he looked at her. She imagined his thick black hair, sleepy eyes, and pouty lips, and then she wondered about Darnell. Was he as stunning as his sister? She had promised Monique that she would keep an eye on Joe, but maybe that wasn't such a good idea.

———

Her efforts to avoid Joe worked until Thursday morning when he knocked on the door to her suite.

"I'm sorry to disturb you, but Libby said you'd be awake." Joe was disheveled again, like he had been when they first met.

Emma clutched at her robe with one hand and raked at her hair with the other.

"Is something wrong?"

"No, I mean there was, but I think now it's okay. I

called Austin's office, and she said this happens sometimes. I soaked the sheets in cold water, but I don't know
if the blood will come out, and I have to get back upstairs,
but I'll need fresh sheets and more of those disposable bed
pads, and I didn't see the woman who makes the beds,
and Libby was busy with breakfast, so…"

"If Dr. Austin's not worried, I'm sure everything is fine.
Go back up to Avi, and I'll be there in a minute."

Emma closed the door. No time for makeup, but she
wasn't about to run upstairs in her nightgown and robe.
She dressed, washed her face, ran a brush through her
hair, rinsed her mouth with mouthwash, then, to avoid
early risers in the dining room, she rushed through the
parlor to the front foyer, then up the stairs. She took clean
sheets and bed pads from the linen closet then found the
door to Joe's room slightly ajar. "Hello…"

"Come in, I'm rinsing out the sheets. They're almost
as good as new."

Emma pushed the door open, but remained standing
in the hall, and watched Joe across the foyer in the bathroom, on his knees, and leaning over the tub—the small
of his back between his T-shirt and jeans exposed.

"I think I got the blood out of the bottom sheet and the
mattress pad." He stood and looked at Emma. "But I'm
more than happy to buy new ones." His T-shirt was wet
and suggested a well-chiseled chest and stomach beneath it.

"No need to buy anything." Emma said. "We're pros at getting stains out of sheets." A blush rose in her neck. "What I mean is, similar accidents have happened before with Dr. Austin's patients."

"We've been using the pads, but I guess Avi turned a little on his side while he was sleeping, and blood leaked out around one of his drains. He's been draining more on the left side than on the right, so we've been emptying the left grenade more often—you know, those bulbs that the drains are attached to."

Emma understood what Joe meant from her conversations with Dr. Austin about her guests' postoperative needs. Dr. Austin had been the one to supply Emma with bed pads to protect mattresses and upholstered furniture.

Beyond the foyer, two beds—a double and a twin—took up much of the room. Avi reclined against a mound of pillows covered with crochet-trimmed pillowcases against the tufted headboard of the twin bed. His slight torso was bare except for bandages wrapped around his chest with the two plastic grenades pinned to the bandages. Plastic tubing extended from each grenade and disappeared under Avi's arms.

Emma slowly stepped into the foyer and saw Avi shifting against the pillows as if trying to find comfort. She lowered her eyes.

In the bathroom, Joe hung the wet sheets over the shower door, while Emma recalled the many times, as a child and then as a young woman, she had scrubbed bedding or upholstery or carpeting to remove her mother's—then later her husband's—stench of alcohol and vomit. Back then, she masked reality with cheap curtains, plastic flowers, knickknacks, and air fresheners, purchased or stolen from flea markets and dollar stores.

"Avi meet Emma," Joe yelled from the bathroom.

Avi looked up from his cell phone, removed his earbuds, and smiled. His features and smile reminded Emma of Monique, but there was also something of Joe in the way Avi's eyes met Emma's. *Adoption or surrogacy?* Emma wondered. She was surprised that Avi neither blushed nor drew his sheet up over the grenades swelling with blood like leeches. Instead he stared into Emma, making *her* feel exposed and vulnerable.

"Hi," he said. "Nice place and the breakfasts are great."

In vain, Emma searched for the perfect words to say as she walked from the foyer into the bedroom, then placed the clean sheets and the pads on the unmade bed. She settled on, "Thank you. I'll make up the bed for you now."

"Sorry about the sheets," Avi said.

"No need to be."

"Let me help," Joe said. He came out of the bathroom buttoning up a dry shirt, and he and Emma stood on either side of the bed, stretching out the bottom sheet and securing the corners, then doing the same with the mattress pad, then the top sheet. The mirror across the room, over the gas fireplace, captured Emma sweeping her hair away from a crimson cheek. The intimacy of the simple act of making the bed had unnerved her.

"Should I bring the wet sheets downstairs?" Joe asked.

"No." Emma cleared her throat. "One of the house-keepers will be up later." She turned to Avi. "Very nice meeting you."

Again, Avi looked up from his cell phone. "Thanks for making the bed."

Scads of get-well cards sat on the dresser. Emma thought to mention them, to say something like *many people must care about you*, but instead she spoke to Joe. "Should I give Libby your breakfast order?"

Joe leaned over Avi and kissed his forehead. "What do you think? Does breakfast in bed sound good? You can skip going to the dining room this morning."

Avi nodded.

"I'll walk downstairs with you," Joe said to Emma.

As they walked, she ran her fingertips along a seam in the wallpaper that had separated. Self conscious, she said, "I tend to obsess about minutia."

"Nothing wrong with caring," Joe said.

Emma remained quiet until they reached the bottom

of the stairs, where she paused. "I have work to do. Have a nice breakfast."

"Thank you," Joe said. "Staying here has made everything much easier."

Emma nodded.

Once behind the heavy door to her suite, Emma wiped a single tear from her cheek. Before Dr. Austin's patients, Emma's guests had been on holiday, and despite occasional complaints about mundane things like room temperature or a television not working, most conversations were pleasant, not delving any deeper than the veneer on an antique chifforobe.

She recalled Dr. Austin's concern that her patients have a safe and comfortable place to recover, and Emma took pride in providing that—but she couldn't shake how fragile Avi appeared, his chest wrapped in bandages, and those awful plastic leeches. Nor could she dismiss the image of Joe in a wet T-shirt, and the envy she felt when Joe so tenderly kissed Avi's forehead.

Emma had long taken an almost smug pride in the way she had reinvented her own life. But had she recovered? Or did she simply bury her past under other people's furnishings—as if through a chair or table or vintage photograph of another mother and daughter or husband and wife, Emma could make everything better?

Emma would have preferred to resume a low profile for another three days, until Joe and Avi checked out; however, the first play of the summer season opened, and every room in the B&B was booked. Late Friday afternoon, instead of tea, Emma hosted a wine and cheese party, early enough to allow her guests time to dine at local restaurants before curtain.

Slices of late-afternoon sunlight shone through the parlor's tall, narrow windows, and Emma tried her best to appear as cool as her pale-green linen tank top and matching slacks. She poured wine and tactfully repeated several times where she had purchased not only the chardonnay and pinot noir but also the crystal stemware.

Among her returning guests, conversation flowed, but for newcomers it was more of a trickle until Emma skillfully engaged everyone, including the most timid, and soon the whole parlor bubbled with small talk.

"Will tonight be the first time you've seen *M. Butterfly*?" asked a man with silver hair and a gold wedding band matching his balding husband's.

"No, no," answered a thin, middle-aged woman. She pointed to a fuller version of herself standing at her side. "My sister and I saw it on Broadway."

Another woman, with a mane of salt and pepper hair and eye shadow the color of sunset extended her fingers as if she were casting a spell. "I adore walking along

Herring Cove in September, taking in the many layers of light."

"Yes, Provincetown reminds me of Venice," one of Emma's favorite returning guests responded. "I've been vacationing there for years. So much water to reflect the sunlight." Ellie was the first guest that Dr. Austin had referred to Emma's. She had lived almost all of her life as male—first as a son, then as a husband and father, then as a widower and grandfather. She was seventy when she transitioned and when Emma first met her, and after that she returned often for extended weekends.

Guests checked the time on their watches and cell phones. En masse, they gathered jackets or sweaters or shawls. Several women clutched small evening purses.

Ellie's was coral satin. She blew a kiss to Emma. "Lovely as always, my dear."

"Enjoy!" Emma repeated numerous times until the last guest closed the front door, and Emma collapsed into a Victorian club chair, kicked off her heels, sighed, and finished her glass of wine. She was lost in random thoughts and beginning to doze when Joe's voice startled her.

"Did we miss a party?" Joe and Avi stood under the arch between the front foyer and parlor. They had just returned from dinner.

Emma sat up and slipped her feet back into her shoes. "Just a little wine and cheese." She extended her hand toward the tiered serving cart. "I believe the chardonnay is gone, but there's pinot noir left, if you'd like."

"That sounds great. Just let me help Avi get settled upstairs." Avi smiled at Emma, then yawned and rubbed his eyes.

As Joe and Avi ascended the stairs, Emma gathered the dirty wine glasses and plates and pushed the cart into the kitchen. She placed an almost full bottle of pinot noir and two wine-glasses on a tray, rearranged the remaining cheese, fruit, and crackers on a smaller plate, and placed the plate, cocktail napkins, and an appetizer fork next to them, then returned to the parlor, placed the tray on the coffee table before the settee, and poured two glasses of wine, making this her third. She sat, glanced around the room, and spotted a few stray napkins. She stood and stashed them in her pocket, then returned to her chair and pretended to scan a magazine.

When Joe finally returned, he took a seat on the settee next to Emma. She noticed a hint of aftershave. His hair was freshly combed.

He lifted one of the glasses of wine. "To you."

"To me?" Emma said and lifted her glass.

"Yes, to someone who makes things better." Joe pointed to the plate of snacks. "Everything you do is perfect. I don't mean just things, but the way you treat your guests. You care. And that makes everything feel better."

"Thank you." Emma sipped her wine and glanced about the room until her eyes fell upon a small painting, a shadowy silhouette of a woman cradling an infant. The painting hung askew on the wall in its gilded frame, above an oak side-by-side. Emma recalled the abortion she had had at fifteen, and the miscarriage at nineteen after one of her husband's many assaults.

"Are you okay?" Joe said.

"Of course." Emma stood, walked to the picture, and straightened it. "One of the silly things I care about." When she returned to the settee, she asked about Avi, mentioning that she thought he looked tired.

"We went out for dinner. I think it did him in."

Emma asked about the restaurant, the menu, the service, and the food, gathering information to update a review, while Joe picked at the grapes and finished his wine.

"More?" Emma said, filling his glass without waiting for him to reply.

She usually drank one glass of wine, never more than two. She nursed her third glass cautiously. "Will he be okay?"

"Avi? Sure. We also went out for an early dinner last night. He was fine after he rested."

"No, I mean will he be okay, *really* okay. Will he be who he wants to be?"

Joe appeared surprised by Emma's question, but no more surprised than she was that she asked it. He sat back and Emma expected to be rebuked for being so presumptuous, but instead she heard, "I don't know." Joe had whispered it so softly that she was unsure if he had said anything at all.

"I wanted him to wait. You know, to be old enough to sign for himself. I didn't think that it was my place to choose this kind of surgery for another person, even if the person was my child, but then I realized that either way I was making a choice. You know what I mean? If I didn't give him my permission to have the top surgery, then I was choosing to prolong his misery." Joe finished his second glass of wine. "Will he be okay? I don't know."

Emma didn't offer to refill his glass. They had both had enough. Joe placed his empty glass on the table, then laced his fingers together and rested his elbows on his knees. "Avi's grandparents disapprove. But they didn't live with him. They didn't see the tears. They weren't there when he'd point at a mirror and scream that he hated what he saw. They didn't climb into bed with him and lay there holding him while he cried himself to sleep."

Joe reached into his hip pocket, pulled out his wallet, opened it to a picture, then held the open wallet out to Emma. "Imagine that. He hated what he saw. I thought *she* was the most beautiful girl in the world, but that was the problem. He didn't want to see a girl in the mirror, because that's not what he was."

Emma took the wallet from Joe. Looking back at her was a stunning girl, about fourteen, with a heart-melting smile. Her hair fell in thick, dark shoulder-length twists, and she wore a yellow tank top.

Emma didn't know what to say. It didn't seem right to compliment the image that gave Avi so much pain. She closed the wallet and placed it on the coffee table.

"When Avi first told me that he was definitely trans-gender—that's how he put it, 'I'm definitely transgender'—I asked what he needed from me, while my head felt as if it might explode. I had lost Darnell a month before, and inside I was a mess, but outside I remained calm. I said, 'What do you need me to do?' He said that he wanted to use male pro-nouns and change his name. His name was Ariella."

"Were you surprised?" It felt like trivial question, but Emma thought she should say something.

"No, I wasn't surprised. I just wanted it to not be true. But then, he didn't want it to be true either. He just want-ed to be what he was supposed to be. A boy."

"You love Avi very much, don't you?" Again, Emma felt that her words sounded trite.

Joe nodded, but remained silent. The light in the tall, narrow windows faded, and even though the lamps weren't lit, Emma could see Joe's eyes moisten. She placed her hand over his clasped hands. She was startled by her spontaneity—yet pleased.

"I don't blame my parents or Darnell's parents. They don't understand. Truth is, neither do I. But it's not about understanding. It's about believing. There were always signs. We thought he was a tomboy, then a lesbian, and then Darnell got sick, very sick. Avi was in middle school at the time, and suddenly he was wearing makeup and obsessing over what to wear to school dances, arguing with us to let him buy slinky dresses and spiked heels, but it didn't make sense. He was like, let me look in the mirror just long enough to put on mascara, and as soon as a school dance was over, he tore off his dress like it was choking him, and scrubbed his face clean. Getting him to pose for pictures was torture. He wasn't being honest; he was just trying to fix things, to make everything better, with clothes and makeup. But he couldn't make himself be a girl any more than he could make Darnell live." Joe opened his hands, then clasped them around Emma's. "Sorry. Guess it's the wine talking."

Emma's breath quickened and her heart raced. Her eyes were riveted on his hands, and she imagined them moving up her arms, to her shoulders, then Joe drawing her to him while their eyes closed. She imagined his lips brushing hers.

Joe's cell phone made a clicking noise. He released Emma's hands and checked his phone. "It's Avi. I promised him I wouldn't be long. We're going to watch *Mean*

Girls for the fifth time. Not sure how many dads routinely watch *Mean Girls* with their sons." Joe chuckled.

Emma sighed. "Good dads would," she said.

Joe stood and took his wallet from the coffee table. He stared at Emma until she lowered her eyes for fear that she might beg him to stay.

"Thank you for the wine and for listening," he said.

She watched him fade into a mélange of shadows, and as he turned into the foyer, Emma recalled Ellie pausing at the same spot and blowing her a kiss. *Lovely, as always, my dear…You make everything perfect.*

Emma stood, hesitant, then carried the tray of empty wine glasses and the plate of cheese back into the kitchen. She placed the dirty glasses and plate on the serving cart with the others, to be washed. She brought her fingertips to her eyes, and she wondered if her tears were for Avi, or Joe, or herself. She sighed and thought of how lovely Ellie had looked and how naturally she clutched her coral evening purse. Emma dried her tears, then returned to the dining room.

On the white board, with a fine-point marker, she carefully wrote out the next day's breakfast menu in meticulous calligraphy: juice, coffee, teas, strawberries in cream, and eggs (your way) or French toast. She used a clear plastic ruler to measure between each word and line. Given the three glasses of wine, it took her a bit longer than usual. She placed the white board on a gilded easel, stood back, tilted her head, then moved the easel—just a tad, until everything was perfect.

Figlio Mio

Nettie presses the tips of her soapy fingers into her left breast. The almond shaped lump is no larger or smaller, but there it is: the hard reminder of the likelihood that eventually, maybe sooner than expected, Gio will be left without her to care for him.

Blind, the doctor said when Gio was born; however, not only could Gio see, but he loved light and color. As a toddler, Gio once reached for Nettie's crystal earrings on a night she and Dominick dressed for the opera. The next morning, Nettie removed every crystal pendant from the dining-room chandelier and hung them in the windows like sparkling teardrops. When sunlight shone through the crystals, the apartment became awash in rainbows, and Gio chirped content, like a chickadee on a warm winter's day.

Deaf, the doctor also said, but that didn't stop Nettie from singing to Gio. She had a beautiful voice. "My own mezzo soprano," her husband, Dominick, would say, and when Nettie sang to Gio, he pressed his ear against her breast, and he sighed deep breaths that sounded like joy.

Finally, the doctor said that Gio would live for only a few years. That was thirty-six years ago. She and Dominick had hoped to be with their son when his end-time came, but Dominick had passed almost ten years ago, and Nettie now feared that she would soon join him. Not an unpleasant thought, except for leaving Gio.

Dominick had called her Antoinette. "You're too pretty for an old-lady nickname," he'd say, especially when they made love.

Nettie steps out of the hot shower and catches her reflection in the mirror as the steam clears. With one hand, she holds the bath towel to her breast, and with her free hand she sweeps her thinning gray hair away from her face and examines another age spot. She's grown into her old-lady nickname and finds life wanting without Dominick.

Gio sits in the hallway outside the bathroom. Nettie had left the door slightly ajar. He wears a harness attached to a leash, which she tied to the radiator in case he became weary of rocking and thought to wander. Deadbolts secure the front and back doors, but there are also dangers inside the house, including small objects, which Gio might try to eat and choke on—even a stray rubber band could be deadly.

At meals, Nettie cuts Gio's food into small pieces and places a few bites at a time on his plate.

Dominick once tried to teach Gio to eat slowly. He placed his hand over Gio's mouth between bites, but Gio became agitated and dug at his nose until it bled. Meals were a terrible ordeal. They discovered that small pieces of soft food, a little at a time, proved to be the only option.

Nettie slips into a housedress, fills the tub for Gio's bath, and then presses her mottled hand against the slightly ajar door. "Come figlio mio." She undoes his harness and undresses him, and he arches his small, frail body backward and blinks at the overhead lights. It's a wonder his tiny spine doesn't splinter like a reed.

As Nettie helps Gio step into the warm bathwater, his hands quiver like the leaves of an aspen. He chirps and lowers his tiny bottom into the tub. Nettie gently rubs the soapy washcloth across his birdlike shoulders.

Gio resembles a character in a macabre Mother Goose nursery rhyme. A mischievous, hairy little gnome, not to be trusted. Even neighbors that Nettie has known since her youth, who have known Gio since he was born, avoid looking upon him, as if he is something to fear rather than someone to cherish.

Nettie rubs a drop of baby shampoo into Gio's patch of black cowlicks, which refuse to lie flat against his tiny scalp. She had never heard of microcephaly until that day in the hospital when the doctor described Gio's condition, and she held her newborn son to her breast, but he refused to suckle. "In time he will," Dominick said.

But the doctor said, "I'm afraid time will not resolve this issue."

And Nettie snapped, "My son is not your issue."

She covers Gio's eyes with a towel and rinses his hair with tepid water. His body tenses, and she knows that he fears his eyes might sting.

"All done, figlio mio," she says and gently lifts his arm. He stands, looks up at the overhead light, flutters his hands, and chirps.

Look at the birds in the air...are you not much more valuable than they? Nettie twists her lips, flares her nostrils, and dismisses her memory of the Bible verse. She once said countless novenas, praying that the Blessed Mother either perform a miracle and cure Gio or take him home to heaven, but neither happened, and in time Nettie prayed less, until her vigil candles went dark, and her religious statues became little more than knickknacks to dust.

She dries Gio, shaves him with shaving cream and a razor (he's afraid of the electric shaver), rubs deodorant under his arms, and dresses him in his best clothes, including a white shirt and a red tie.

She finds her daughter Josie sitting at the kitchen table doing a crossword puzzle. Josie, her husband, and her children live in the apartment upstairs. She favors

Dominick—not pretty like Nettie once was, but she's a handsome woman, and her yellow blouse compliments her olive complexion and dark brown hair. Her height and strong features can be intimidating, especially when she flashes her dark eyes and arches her eyebrows. But Nettie is not easily intimidated, and when Josie grows impatient or testy, Nettie barks, "Don't forget I once changed your diapers."

Josie answers, "And someday I'll change yours."

Nettie laughs and waves her hand, dismissing her daughter's insolence.

"There's fresh coffee on the stove," Nettie says. "Here, watch your brother while I get dressed. Don't let him get dirty. That's his only white shirt."

"He looks handsome," Josie says.

Nettie looks at her daughter and son—one formidable, one fragile. *Josie could care for Gio*, she thinks, and though comforted by the thought, she neither expects nor wants it to happen. Josie has three children. Actually, worse than children—teenagers, and her husband doesn't lift a finger around the house. No, Gio is a mother's responsibility, not a sister's. Nettie sighs, but not the joyful way Gio sighs when she sings to him as he presses his ear to her breast.

An outspoken cousin once suggested that Nettie *put Gio away*. Nettie responded, "You put clothes away, not children."

156

"You have another child to think of. Is it fair to Josie?" her cousin said.

"And who made you the patron saint of fairness?" Nettie bristled. She never spoke to that cousin again.

Nettie's parents were from the old country—a small town outside of Palermo, Sicily—and Nettie espoused many of their provincial ways, including a mistrust of strangers.

She changes into a navy blue with white polka dots taffeta dress that whispers when she walks. She brushes her hair and spots Dominick admiring her from his picture on the dresser. He always complimented Nettie when she wore this dress, and she can hear "My beautiful Antoinette," as her taffeta skirt rustles against her nylon slip. She smiles back at him through the mirror's reflection. "It's our anniversary, Dominick. Josie is driving me and Gio to the cemetery." She doesn't tell him about the lump.

In the kitchen, Josie holds a small battery-operated fan before Gio's face, and his hands rest in her lap, his fingers slightly curled like the petals of a lily. He turns his head from left to right and back again in slow, rhythmic movements, as if he feels music in the fan's breeze. Nettie's dress announces her entrance, but she doesn't speak; her children look so peaceful, and she recalls a time when Gio was no trouble at all, before he went from crawling to climbing to running and then shoving small objects into his mouth. If he choked, Dominick would

157

pick him up, turn him upside down, and pat his back until whatever had stuck in his throat was dislodged. In time the family all learned the Heimlich, even the grandchildren. A poster showing the procedure hung like an omen on the refrigerator door.

Not long after Gio started to walk and then run (at about three years old) a woman entered Dominick and Nettie's bakery with her toddler on a leash. "He's very active," the woman said, sounding apologetic. "In a split second, he pulls away from me and runs into the street."

Nettie asked the woman where she had bought the harness and leash, and the next morning she bought one of each. They gave her a little peace of mind while she cooked or cleaned, attended to her personal needs, or worked in the kitchen behind the bakery. She was very conscious not to overuse the leash—and she would never use it in public; strangers already looked at Gio as if he were a wild animal. But without it, Nettie might have yielded to her critics' opinions, and "put Gio away." Bright lights, soft stuffed animals, feathers, or the breeze from a fan occupied Gio for short chunks of time, but there was no way Nettie could watch Gio every second of the day, and it took only a second for Gio to choke.

———

"This way," Josie says, and they follow her past rows of gravestones and across yellow, brittle grass. Josie carries a spray of flowers adorned with the words 'Anniversary in Heaven,' and Nettie holds Gio's hand, sweat pooling where their fingers lace. Gio arches his neck and blinks up at a crow circling above them—an ominous blue-black specter against the sun-parched sky. Nettie sneers at the crow and extends the pinky and index fingers of her free hand downward in the shape of horns to ward off the crow's evil eye.

An elderly man, filling an empty coffee can at a spigot, glances at Gio and smiles at Nettie, but she returns his smile with a curt nod, then takes an embroidered handkerchief smelling of Jean Nate from her purse and pats Gio's brow. Gio sniffs at the air.

Josie strides across graves, and Nettie stops and wipes perspiration from her neck. "I should have brought roller skates." She tucks the handkerchief in her belt.

"We're almost there," Josie says.

"I know where your father's grave is. Why are you in such a hurry? He's not going anywhere."

Gio chirps, shakes his head, and thumps his fingers against his cheek.

Josie pauses and waits for Nettie and Gio. Together they approach the small headstone with the surname "Dolci" bracketed by etchings of sunflowers—Dominick's favorite. He once grew them and dried the seeds for the birds that visited his garden, and in winter he filled feeders outside their kitchen windows so Gio could chirp at the birds year round. Underneath "Dolci" is the name Dominick and the dates of his birth and death. When Nettie purchased the stone and met with the etcher, he offered to add her name and the date of her birth at a discount. She said, "Could I get another discount if we guess when I'm gonna die?" The poor man blushed, and Josie rolled her eyes and apologized for her mother.

"I don't know if this is going to work," Josie says as she tries to press the spray's metal prongs into the bone-dry earth. "The dirt is like a rock."

Gio pulls at Nettie's hand and sways from one foot to the other. "Here, hold your brother's hand. Lemme try."

"Ma, how are you going to…"

But Nettie insists, and Josie yields to her mother's demands while Nettie rummages through her purse, retrieves the coupon insert from Sunday's newspaper, spreads it out on the grass, and kneels next to the headstone. She also finds a stainless steel nail file, and chips away at the top layer of dirt until she's able to secure the spray's prongs.

"Good! Now it won't blow away." But Nettie's knees and back have gone stiff, and she struggles to stand. Gio appears distracted by the sunlight reflecting off the headstone, so Josie releases his hand and helps Nettie to her feet.

"Stubborn as a mule!" Josie says.

Nettie puffs and leans against the headstone. "I'm fine. Take Gio back to the car. You can sit in the air conditioning.

I need to talk to your father."

"Don't be long. It's too hot for you to stand out here."

"So I'll sit." Nettie plops her white polka-dotted bottom atop the headstone as Josie shakes her head, takes Gio's hand, and heads back to the car.

Wiping her hand across her forehead, and then brushing grass from her skirt, Nettie's thoughts drift to a long-ago hot summer evening, when she and Dominick sat in their yard, under the arbor, and Gio stared up into the colored lights strung through the grapevines, sniffing the sweetness of grapes and citronella. Dominick poured Nettie a glass of homemade wine, and she prepared a plate for him—ricotta salata and slices of fresh-picked peaches and pears, from their fruit trees. A blue jay pecked at Dominick's dried sunflower seeds, in harmony with the clink of Nettie and Dominick's wine glasses.

"Salute!" A few drops of wine splattered on the picnic table. "Happy anniversary, cara mia."

A headstone makes for an uncomfortable seat, and there's no arbor with grapevines to provide shelter for Nettie on this hot afternoon, but none of this matters when Nettie visits with Dominick.

Josie's a good daughter, Dominick. Made us crazy when she was a teenager, but what teenager doesn't make their parents crazy? Now, I don't know what I'd do without her.

Maybe they were right, Dominick. About finding a place for Gio to live. Maybe it wasn't fair to Josie. Maybe it's still not.

Nettie reaches into her purse in search of something: a stray peppermint; rosary beads, although she no longer prays the rosary; or maybe a tissue. She shakes her head, pulls the Jean Nate handkerchief from her belt, wipes her face and neck, and then places the damp handkerchief in her purse.

Remember, Dominick, that time when we visited the new Developmental Center? It was after Mamma got sick, and she could no longer help with Gio. He was about twelve. I told you that I wasn't signing no papers––that I was just looking––like you would ever make me to do anything I didn't want to do. It looked like an octopus sitting on that hillside next to the zoo. What a place to build it. Animals in cages next to people in cages. I know the people weren't in cages, but it felt like it.

Remember all those long, white cinderblock hallways? Cold looking, but a nice young man––hardly a man––answered the buzzer to the unit where Gio would live. He looked like Jesus. Back then all the boys looked like Jesus, and the girls looked like Mary Magdalene with their wild hair and bangles. His name was Carmine. Remember? Nice boy. He showed us around the unit. They tried to make it look homey with pictures and plastic flowers.

There was one old man––not sure why he was there, all the other residents were young. Remember they called them "residents"? Carmine said it was better than saying "patients." The old man slumped in a wheelchair next to a metal screen. He held out one hand and made a scissors motion with his fingers, then pressed his forehead against the screen.

I can still smell Pine Sol and the stink of overcooked food in steam tables. "Pane!" the man shouted. He looked like a prize-fighter, with his puffy eyelids and cauliflower ears. Like your cousin Benny. I told Carmine that pane means bread, but he already knew that. He said that Mr. DiPalma was more interested in amore than pane. He said that Mr. DiPalma had a thing for one of the food servers. I liked that he called the man Mr. DiPalma. He showed respect.

Nettie bends, picks up the coupon insert, and shades her eyes with it. She looks toward Josie's car, and wonders if Josie is growing impatient, or worried. She shrugs. Talking to Dominick is more important. She rests the insert on her head like a paper hat, and leans again against the gravestone.

Maybe the place wasn't so bad. I had to chuckle when that boy ran out, looking so proud of himself. Just a little older than Gio. His hair was wet, and he wore a nice blue button-down shirt, but nothing else. Remember? He carried his pants and underpants, and he made a trail of wet footprints behind him.

Carmine was very polite. He lowered the boy's hands to cover the boy's private parts and called someone to help him dress. Myrtle was her name. She was nice too. Remember? A black woman. Very pretty. She had an Afro. That's what Josie said they call that hairdo. You know, like a halo. Remember, she had kind eyes like

163

an angel? She held another boy's hand. He was tall and hand-some, but he had a funny walk and held one arm close to his chest. Carmine said the two boys had just moved to the Developmental Center. He said that they grew up in a backward and were still adjusting. I didn't know what a backward was, but it didn't sound like anything I'd want to know about.

"Ma!"

Nettie looks up. Her hair is wet, her dress sticks to her back, and she sees Josie standing next to the car. Nettie stands but falters, and leans back against the headstone until Josie reaches her.

Josie grabs Nettie's arm. "Just give me a minute," Nettie says.

"I told you it was too hot, but of course you wouldn't listen."

Nettie ignores Josie's comment. "Where's your brother?"

"He's in the car. I locked the door."

"In this heat?" Nettie shouts.

"The air conditioning is on."

"So you left the car running with him in it?"

Josie lets go of her mother's arm, and Nettie grabs the headstone to steady herself.

"What the hell do you expect me to do? I can't take care of both of you. I have enough children. I don't need anymore." Josie clenches her fists and takes a deep breath. "Can we please just walk back to the car?"

Nettie stiffens when Josie touches her, but she knows she has no choice but to lean on her daughter. They walk back to the car in silence and find Gio sitting in the back seat tapping his fingers against his cheek.

"Fasten your seatbelt," Josie tells her mother, as she removes the wet newspaper from her head.

Even before they left the cemetery, Nettie was already lost in her thoughts, as if the harsh words she exchanged with Josie were merely an unpleasant breech in her visit with Dominick.

Maybe that wouldn't have been such a bad place for Gio to live. But then we went in that smaller room, and there was that boy watching television. He rocked back and forth and sounded like he was snoring. He popped up like a jack-in-the-box and hugged Carmine, and then let go of him, walked back to his chair and rocked back and forth some more. He looked like the strong man in the circus, and he had the same puffy eyelids and cauliflower ears like Mr. DiPalma. I was glad when Carmine asked us to wait in the other room.

When Carmine came back out, I asked him why Mr. Di-Palma and that boy looked like prizefighters. All he said was "uncontrolled seizures." I felt terrible for them, but I was afraid that boy could break Gio in half if he got mad at him.

And then we went out on the patio where boys and girls sat together. The girls lived next door. It was hot, like today, and some of them sat around a table under a large umbrella; two boys sat in wheelchairs, and one, a little older, paced back and forth shouting, "I'm a mechanical!" Carmine explained that it was getting close to lunchtime and the boy was probably hungry. "Mechanical" was the word they used for food that was ground in a blender, for people who don't chew good. I figured they'd do the same thing with Gio's food. The boy pacing back and forth had a sunken mouth like he was toothless.

Then, one of the workers––she had a long braid, blue-jean shorts, and a tiny tie-dye top––took a heavy resident's baby doll away from her. The resident might have been about eighteen. She wore a flowered sundress. The worker said, "I found your purse." I think the resident's name was Harriet. She handed Harriet the purse, instead of her baby doll, but I could see Harriet was mad.

I must have made a face, because Carmine said something about it being more appropriate for a young woman to hold a purse than a baby doll. He said they call it "normalization," but I couldn't hold my tongue, and I said, "More appropriate for who? For a girl to sit all dressed up in a party dress rocking a purse instead of a doll while she waits for a bus that never comes?"

You told me to hush, Dominick, but of course I didn't. "Maybe someone should tell that employee that it would be more appropriate if she wore a bra instead of jiggling all over the place," I said. I could see the worker heard me. I was just looking for a fight, so I could walk out thinking it was a terrible place, but Carmine stayed calm. He said that they take the residents out a lot, and he sees how the outside world looks at them, and he said that the residents probably see it too.

"Maybe these little efforts around appearances, though they might seem silly or even a little cruel, will spare them unkind glances. Maybe our residents will be a little more accepted," he said. He had a nice way of talking. Remember?

He was probably right, but I wouldn't admit it. Didn't I get Gio all dressed up today? And who was gonna see Gio in a cemetery? A ghost? Carmine was like you, Dominick—calm and patient.

Nettie nods, as if agreeing with her memory. She closes her eyes and finds Dominick's smile.

In the vegetable garden, you held your hands over Gio's and showed him how to pull weeds, and he pulled weeds. And in the bakery, you held your hands over Gio's, and showed him how to knead dough, and he kneaded dough. You were patient with Gio and with Josie and with me, and eventually with our grandchildren, when they were little. Maybe Carmine and Myrtle could have taught Gio more. Maybe it would have been a good place for him to live.

But I couldn't do it. I imagined them taking Gio's stuffed animals away, or the fur collar I gave him from my old winter coat, or the feathers he stroked against his cheek; and handing him a briefcase instead, and maybe putting lifts in his shoes to make him taller, or covering his small head with a fedora. I wanted to smack that worker for taking away Harriet's doll.

When we left, you didn't ask me what I thought. You knew the answer. We never even talked about it. We just drove home and acted like we had never gone there. So now I'm talking about it, Dominick. Now we have to talk about it.

Nettie fears she might cry.

"Do you need to stop for groceries before we go home?" Josie says.

Nettie looks at her daughter as if she's surprised to find Josie sitting next to her. She shakes her head no, turns away, looks out the window, and notices a crossing guard holding up her hand and a line of young children crossing the street in front of their car. Nettie covers her mouth to stifle a sob.

Dominick, I have a hard lump in my breast. What's gonna happen to Gio?

———

Nettie stares at the television without paying attention, reads newspapers without understanding them, cleans her spotless apartment, organizes her already organized closets and drawers, irons, mends, and weeds, while Gio pets his stuffed animals, or runs feathers along the inside of his arms, or rocks from one foot to the other in the backyard while he blinks at the sky. Nettie's grandchildren ask her what's wrong, and she responds with, "Take out the garbage," or "Go to store," or "Move the laundry from the washer to the dryer." Soon, they leave her alone, which is exactly what she wants.

She dreams about Carmine. In her dreams, she and Dominick still own the bakery, and Carmine comes in to buy cannoli and sfogliatella. Nettie places the pastries in a box, and after she ties the box with string, she brings Carmine's hand to her breast so he will understand, but then Carmine becomes Dominick, and Nettie wakes with Dominick's name on her lips. Sometimes Carmine orders different pastries, or a loaf of semolina bread, but it always ends with Nettie waking and calling out to Dominick.

As the days pass, Nettie becomes more silent. She speaks only when spoken to, and her answers are brief.

Finally Josie confronts her. "Ma, something is wrong. What is it? Are you still angry because I yelled at you in the cemetery? It was hot. We both got irritable."

Nettie cleans the crystal pendants that hang in the windows. She puts down the Windex and paper towel and looks at her daughter.

"Josie, did I do wrong by you?"

"What are you talking about?" Josie says.

"Keeping Gio home. Was that the wrong thing to do?"

"That's water under the bridge," Josie says.

"Yes, I guess it is." Nettie resumes cleaning.

"Maybe it was wrong," Josie says, "but that's in the past. It's now we have to figure out."

Nettie runs the damp paper towel along another crystal,

while a light rain streaks tears on the kitchen windows, and Gio taps his pinky and thumb against the pane.

Josie talks to the back of her mother's head, and then finally says, "I'll be down later, and we'll have coffee."

That evening, before Nettie and Gio sit down for dinner, she hands Gio plates, then silverware, then napkins, and he sets the table for dinner—one item at a time—running his hand along the cool of the enamel top to feel where to place each item. Nettie has made penne with meat sauce, and she cuts a few penne into tiny pieces, and then smashes a meatball into it. She spoons a little onto Gio's plate, then little more, and a little more, but she barely touches her own food. She's had very little appetite since discovering the lump in her breast.

She remembers that Josie had mentioned that a friend of hers said that things have changed, that there are many services that didn't exist before—people can help out in your home, and there are smaller residential settings, not just big institutions. Nettie thought it curious that Josie had talked with a friend about this, as if she sensed something was wrong. Regardless, if something were to happen to Nettie, she already knew that Josie wouldn't—couldn't—care for Gio. And no matter what the size of the residence, Gio would be cared for by strangers. Nettie knew only too well how strangers looked at Gio.

Lost in thought, Nettie stands to carry Gio's empty plate and cup to the sink.

At the familiar sound of Gio gagging, Nettie freezes before the sink and remembers that she had left her plate of food on the table. Next there's the sound of a chair crashing to the floor and Nettie knows Gio is flailing his arms and digging at his nose. She knows his hands are covered in blood, but she doesn't turn around. Instead, she holds her breath and closes her eyes. In a moment it will be all over. Gio will be free. No stranger will ever hurt him, and Josie will not be left with the responsibility and guilt. She's already had too much of that.

Nettie is startled by the gentle caress of a hand on her shoulder, and she spins around, but no one is there. She runs to Gio, stands behind him, clasps her arms around him, and presses her fist up under his tiny sternum until a chunk of meatball dislodges, and Gio gasps. Nettie collapses onto a kitchen chair and sobs.

Gio sucks in slow, deep breaths, and once calm, he strokes Nettie's cheek. He smears his blood with her tears, and then he wraps his arms around the back of her neck and presses his cheek against hers.

The rain has stopped, and the sun, low in the sky, shines through the newly cleaned crystals hanging in the kitchen's westerly windows. Rainbows wash over them, and Gio stretches his tiny, blood-wet fingers up into the colors and chirps.

I know, Dominick. It's not up to me. I'm not God. With that thought, Nettie recalls seeing the crow in the cemetery two weeks ago.

She hugs Gio. "Mamma has to go to the doctor tomorrow. It will be all right. You'll see. It will be all right."

Through her tears she finds the strength to sing, and Gio presses his tiny head against her breast and sighs a joyful sound.

Lila's Cinema

Lila packed her clothes, a few toiletries, vintage movie posters, and several large boxes of DVDs. Her children decided which furniture she should take—little would fit in the small two-room suite. When one of her daughters suggested that Lila choose a favorite chair or end table or comforter, Lila replied, "What a lovely idea." She absent-mindedly pointed to a few items, and when her other daughter suggested that she take family photographs, Lila blushed and said, "Of course, how silly of me to forget."

The staff at Ocean View Senior Living Community marveled at how quickly Lila adjusted to the unfamiliar environment and routines. Unlike most new residents, who were often sullen and had to be cajoled out of their rooms, Lila made a seamless transition from one life stage to the next; in no time, she'd charmed the staff and residents, and when in the company of those who pined about the past—longing for, yet complaining about family—she displayed credible concern, but quickly, graciously redirected the conversation.

"That hairstyle is very becoming on you," or "A simple dress is best. You can always accessorize," or "Did anyone ever tell you that you resemble Vivian Leigh?"

Two weeks after Labor Day and almost two years after Lila moved to Ocean View, she sits on the boardwalk, where the maintenance crew sets out a line of deck chairs. Lila wears a wide-brimmed floppy hat with a black ribbon and large sunglasses to protect her from the sun, and though the ocean breeze is warm, she—like most of the elders enjoying the warm September day—also wears a sweater. Lila's is sequined with mother of pearl buttons.

Summer lingers in the surf, and Lila's own long-distant summers rise like the tide in search of healing: her mother's illness, then a long hospital stay, and finally the night her father said, "Mommy's gone home to God."

She's caught in an undertow of memories when she hears, "Lila, you have a guest." She looks up, and through her dark sunglasses, she sees two haloed silhouettes.

One of the silhouettes says, "I'll leave you to visit with your grandmother."

Grandmother? Lila thinks.

It's been several months since family visited. Lila's children consider their mother to be neither sentimental nor nostalgic, and they see little need for frequent visits. Not that they think of her as cold. Reserved, distant, sometimes aloof, but not cold. Someone, or something to be regarded—not touched—like a bauble in a curio. Maternal? Well not according to Hallmark, which makes it difficult to select Mother's Day cards, but she is amenable, so her move to Ocean View Senior Residence was painless for all involved. Lila's family communicates with her mostly through cards, letters, and the occasional phone call.

"Grandma, it's me. Olive."

Lila looks over her sunglasses, but that doesn't help. Olive sits on the deck chair next to her.

"That's better," Lila says. "I can see you more clearly now. The sun is very bright today. Not complaining. Just saying. But how nice to see you, dear."

"I had an appointment in Manhattan, and I thought— why not just hop on the Long Island Railroad and visit with my grandmother? Mother said it was a good idea, but she wanted me to call first. I called your number, but there was no answer. And I was already at Penn Station, so I just bought a ticket and took a chance. Was it wrong of me to just show up?"

Lila presses her manicured fingernail against the dial on her hearing aid to hear Olive above the bickering seagulls on the beach. "Of course not, dear. I'm glad you came."

But Lila is a bit taken aback, not only by Olive's unexpected arrival, but also by her nervous chattiness—as if she's auditioning for a role as granddaughter rather than actually being one.

Olive wears a thin-strapped cotton summer dress and sits poised but comfortable. She runs her fingers through her blue-black, shoulder length curls, and her dangling earrings reflect the sunlight. *A Hedy Lamarr likeness*, Lila thinks. *Surprising, since her mother resembles Zazu Pitts, and I'm more a June Allyson type. Must be her father's genes.* But there is something familiar about Olive, and Lila can't quite place it.

"Olive, you're absolutely stunning." Lila says. She can't recall how long it's been since she's seen her, but Olive no longer dons earphone appendages, a bull-nose ring, and mini barbells in her earlobes, and she's clearly no longer sullen. *A remarkable transformation*, Lila thinks.

"Thank you, Grandma." A blush rises in Olive's milk-white complexion, and she lowers her eyelids. Her long lashes give her a dreamy, ethereal appearance.

She's a natural, but why on earth did my daughter name this lovely girl Olive? Then Lila remembers that as a baby Olive had been rather round and sour. *But then what baby isn't?*

"Unfortunately, you just missed lunch," Lila says.

"Oh that doesn't matter. I came to see you and to tell you something special before Mother does."

"Well, I haven't spoken with your mother in a while. How are your mother and father? And your sisters? How *are* your sisters and the babies?"

"Oh, they're all fine, but let's not talk about them. Grandma, I came here to thank you."

"Thank me?" Lila says. "For what? I haven't done anything." Lila pulls at her skirt to cover her knees, and then she folds her hands. Something about Olive's youthful sparkle makes her self-conscious.

"Of course you have," Olive says. "You've had a tremendous influence on me."

Influence? Lila thinks. She's guardedly amused at the possibility, given that she had long relinquished the hope of influencing anyone in her family—after too many carefully planned dinners went cold while her husband lingered in front of the television and her children dallied in their bedrooms, and after too many of her new outfits or knickknacks or draperies went unnoticed, but especially after Lila was told once too often to be practical, first by her husband, but eventually by her children. No, real-life marriage and motherhood had proved wanting to Lila: too messy, unlike the final cuts of Hollywood movies, especially her treasured screwball comedies of the '30s and '40s, where scenes resembling real life were left strewn across the editors' floors. A final cut of her marriage, motherhood, and ultimately grand- and great-grand-motherhood might splice together a few hours of delight; editing out the dishes, diapers, and drudgery took too much energy. Lila had kept an immaculate home, prepared tasty meals, did up her hair and makeup to a T, wore stylish clothes, and always pampered her family, but her efforts were performance—worthy of an Oscar, but performance nonetheless. However, at her husband's funeral, when the priest said, "May the souls of the faithful departed rest in peace," and the mourners responded, "Amen!" Lila's *Amen* had the cadence of *It's about time*, much more authentic than her long ago *I do*. Her husband—his belt unbuckled, pants unfastened, and snoring in his recliner—had resembled Anthony Quinn more than Cary Grant. With the exception of Zorba, Lila never cared for Anthony Quinn.

Lila's magazine slips from her lap onto the boardwalk.

Olive picks it up and places it on the bench between them. Martha Stewart looks up at them from its cover.

"Did I say something wrong?" Olive says.

"Oh, no, dear. Quite the contrary. I just never thought of myself as influencing anyone." Lila rearranges her wide-brimmed hat.

Olive leans in closer to her grandmother, as if she's about to tell her a secret. "But you're the reason I'm here, I mean the reason I had a meeting." She lowers her voice, making it difficult for Lila to hear her, and again Lila presses her fingernail against the dial on her hearing aid.

"I want to be the first to tell you," Olive says. "I've been accepted at Juilliard."

Lila repeats, "Juil…li…ard," savoring every syllable.

"I know. Isn't it wonderful, Grandma?"

"Congratulations, dear. I always knew you'd accomplish marvelous things." But Lila knew no such thing.

"I owe my acting and Juilliard to you, Grandma."

"Nonsense, I was a housewife. Hardly a muse for a budding actress." Lila shifts on the bench, crosses her legs, and again pulls at her skirt.

"But you planted the seeds," Olive insists.

"Me? Seeds? I don't even like gardening." Lila chuckles.

"I'm being serious, Grandma."

"Yes, I can see that, dear. No more jesting. Promise." She glances at Martha Stewart's picture as if for advice on how to converse with such a bubbly granddaughter.

"Do you remember that time in Barnes and Noble? We had Italian sodas in the café, and then you said I could choose something to buy."

"Can you be more specific, dear? Remember, I raised four children and have seven grandchildren. Not to mention the great-grandbabies."

"It was when I was in first grade—maybe the first week of school. I wanted a CD instead of a book. Remember? I asked the cashier in the music department if she had any

CDs by Nathan Detroit. Another older woman overheard me and said, 'You mean Frank Sinatra. He played Nathan Detroit in *Guys and Dolls*.' She was quite impressed that I'd know of Nathan Detroit. Remember? She asked you if I was your granddaughter."

Lila searches for the right response. A tiny fib seems fitting. "Of course I remember. No wonder you got into Juilliard. It's because you're so bright, not because of me."

"But I knew about Nathan Detroit because of you. I'm sure I was the only first-grader in my school, probably in the country, that knew so much movie trivia. But it was more than the trivia. You showed me a world of characters and stories—it was a world that no one else my age knew about. And it was more than that. You showed me that when the world isn't beautiful, we could make it beautiful. It wasn't just the movies, Grandma. It was you." Olive spreads out her arms as if she's about to break into song.

Behind her sunglasses, Lila's eyes shift toward the ocean, and she's again caught in an undertow of memories. The girl Lila sits in a dark movie theater; her heart quickens at the resonance of running scales and quivering tremolos; her small fingers cling to her father's arm, and a black-and-white film appears on a large screen. Next, her father sits at her bedside and she tastes salty tears as her father's fingertips smooth back her hair. He whispers that tomorrow she'll go to work with him. *The movie has a happy ending*, he whispers.

"Grandma?"

Lila's voice has the distant sound of the surf. "Did you know my father was a projectionist?"

"Yes," Olive says.

Lila looks at her grandaughter. "When I was a child I hid in the closet so I wouldn't have to attend my own mother's funeral."

Olive's eyes widen and her lips part, but she remains silent.

"My father opened the closet door, and he squatted down in front of me. I can still smell his Bay Rum cologne." Lila smiles and, though she continues to look at Olive, her vision turns inward and she struggles to keep her footing in the undertow. "'You stay here as long as you need,' he said. 'I'll be back in a few hours, and we'll do something special.' A neighbor stayed with me and, when my father returned, he took me to where he worked. But it wasn't like movie theaters today. He worked at the Lowes Valencia, and whenever I was there I felt like a princess. Did I ever tell you about the Valencia Theater?"

"No, Grandma. But Mother said that your father worked there."

"Oh, it was grand. More of a palace than a theater. And so exotic. Like traveling the Mediterranean: Spain, Italy, Morocco, all in one magnificent building. Red carpets, mirrors, fountains, marble and tile floors; elaborate columns painted gold, and lit with chandeliers and sconces. No way I can explain it all, but just one more thing." Lila pauses as if searching for the perfect words. "A backdrop of golden villas covered the walls on each side of the actual theater—not the lobby but the auditorium—and a mural of a blue sky with puffy white clouds masked the ceiling. When the lights dimmed, hundreds of stars shone above and the colorful villas became warm, embracing shadows." Lila brings her fingertips to her face and as she presses her cheeks, her skin ripples like the outgoing tide. She's unaware that words continue to spill from her lips. "I felt like a princess. Nothing could harm me. Not even losing my mother."

Lila wonders why her granddaughter looks so sad.

Olive wipes a tear from her cheek. "I didn't know, Grandma. I'm so very sorry."

Sorry? Lila thinks. She rallies and flutters her fingers as if shoeing away a pesky bug, and then places a hand against the back of her hat. "Fiddle-dee-dee. I don't know why I thought of that. It was so long ago. Just an old woman's rambling. Must be sitting in the sun too long."

"It is hot, Grandma. Would you like a drink of water or something?"

"That would be wonderful, dear." Lila appreciates the respite and hopes that Olive doesn't stay too long. She removes her sunglasses. The beach is deserted except for a man walking hand-in-hand with a small child. More silhouettes.

Lila wonders why she told Olive about her mother. She's not one to talk about such things. Her children knew that her mother had died when she was young, and that ten years later her father also died, but that was enough information. Why trouble them with the unhappy details?

After graduating from high school, Lila worked at the concession stand in the same theater where her father had worked, and not long after he died, she met her husband over a bag of popcorn. Her children knew about this and that they married shortly afterward, but what her children didn't know was that Lila had agreed to marriage because she was very young and feared another good-bye. To Lila's children, the way their parents met and the short courtship sounded romantic, but for Lila it was more about survival than romance—and marriage soon extinguished whatever romance might have existed.

Lila's father had been a generous man, not only with his meager earnings but also in spirit; however, Lila's husband was nothing like her father. Though he provided for his family, he constantly complained about money. When he came home from work, he expected a good meal, a newspaper, television, and not to be bothered. He was a hard worker, but he gave little of himself at home. Lila traded living alone for loneliness with another.

Olive taps Lila's wrist. "Sorry. I didn't mean to startle you."

They're silent while Lila sips her water and exchanges smiles with the elderly couple strolling by, arm in arm.

Finally Olive says, "Grandma, I'm not sure if Mother ever mentioned this to you, but I went through some hard stuff when I started high school."

Lila knows about this. Her daughter had confided in her that Olive was cutting, but Lila's not about to betray her daughter's confidence, and what good would it do to bring all of this up now?

"Becoming a young woman is a difficult time, dear. And your generation has been exposed to too..." Lila pauses. "Well...let's just say too much reality. Reality is overrated. Don't you think? Even the concept of reality shows. Why watch television?"

The corners of Olive's lips curve and her eyes shine. "You're too much, Grandma. Who writes your lines?"

"What do you mean, dear?"

"Oh. Nothing. But you're right, reality *is* overrated. When I was going through...as you say, that difficult time, your house and your movies were my sanctuary. I just want you to know how much it meant to me. How much you mean to me. Watching Frank Sinatra and Ava Gardner and Clark Gable and Bette Davis and all those larger-than-life stars in larger-than-life stories may very well have saved my life. No, it was sitting next to you while watching those movies and laughing, crying, talking, but mostly being quiet. It was all very healing."

May very well have saved my life. Lila contemplates those words. And one of her memories escapes as a tear from the corner of her eye and forms a rivulet down a crease in her cheek. Olive leans forward and caresses her grandmother's hand—an awkward move for both of them.

"I'm sorry, Grandma. I didn't mean to make you sad. I just wanted you to know…."

Lila interrupts her granddaughter. "I know, dear." She sees something of herself in Olive. Not Olive's appearance, but her posture and mannerisms, and something about her diction and the intonation of her voice. Lila's long felt as if she were a stranger in her family, and this sudden and unexpected connection baffles her.

Olive releases Lila's hand, and Lila pulls a tissue from her sleeve. "You know, Olive, your grandfather was a good man and my children were good children. I was a lucky woman. Maybe I didn't know how lucky."

"Maybe they didn't know how lucky they were and still are to have you."

Lila is startled but also moved by Olive's comment.

"Look at what you've done here," Olive says. "I just saw the sign in the parlor. Lila's Cinema! And mom said that the aides are always praising you for the positive impact you've had on the people living here. Mom told them that you've always had a knack for making things special."

When Lila first moved to Ocean View, movie nights were sparsely attended and received snoring ovations, but Lila's DVDs, more varied and in better condition than the quick picks overworked staff checked out of local libraries, changed all that. Within two weeks after Lila's arrival, on Monday and Thursday evenings, folding chairs, wheelchairs, and walkers crowded the larger of two common parlors, and the alert, chatty audience savored Lila's selections—giggling and bantering as Claudette Colbert lifted her skirt and exposed a bit of leg in *It Happened One Night* or Katharine Hepburn and Cary Grant sparred in *The Philadelphia Story* or Carole Lombard threw hissy fits in *Twentieth Century*. Before each film, Lila shared related movie tidbits—a mix of fact and fabrication. She was an aficionado of movie trivia and had a knack for making even the mundane sound thrilling. Vintage movies worked magic—better than Xanax. Snappy quips and laughter soothed feelings of loss and failing bodies, and though reality snaked through the audience and struck without warning—a sudden pain or moment of confusion—it was kicked aside by Astaire's drag step, diminished by Garbo's beauty, or upstaged by Mae West's double entendres.

Lila designed weekly themes according to genre or year

of film release, but the catchiest themes were based on actors. During Joan Crawford week, women painted their lips, penciled their eyebrows, and padded their shoulders. During Lana Turner week, they wore cardigan sweaters backward, and small-breasted women stuffed Depends in their bras, while large-breasted women proudly shortened their bra straps—enduring shoulder pain and backaches for the duration of the movie. Men wore fedoras and bowlers and occasionally sported ascots and monocles. Regular visitors left Ocean View with lists of clothing and accessories to buy at flea markets and secondhand shops. Photographs of silver screen icons and movie posters replaced pictures of rose-covered cottages and stuffed animals on the walls in common areas. The staff and residents called Monday and Thursday's movie nights Lila's Cinema, and Lila felt appreciated—something she never felt during all her years as wife and mother.

"Your mother said I made things special?" Lila says.

Olive seems confused by her grandmother's surprise. "Why wouldn't Mom say that? It's true. You've always fussed over us. Your house was always just so. Holidays were like something out of a storybook." Olive picks up the magazine with the picture of Martha Stewart on its cover. "Compared to you she's a slacker."

Lila finds it difficult to believe Olive's compliment. Expecting her family to come to the kitchen or dining room table for meals felt like a chore, as if she were intruding upon them, and once the kids were out of the house she gave up and bought snack tables, and her husband went from work to his recliner in front of the television; after he retired, the recliner became his Naugahyde appendage. By the time grandchildren came along, her family might have appreciated Lila's efforts on holidays, but by then Lila had long relinquished any hopes for gratitude.

An octogenarian in a wheelchair, pushed by a younger version of himself, calls out to Lila. "Look what my son brought me." He holds up a black, shiny top hat. "It's for tonight's movie." Later, he'll attend Lila's Cinema, first row as always, but until then he and his son join the other slow-moving silhouettes ambling along the boardwalk.

"See, Grandma," Olive whispers. "You're still making magic."

"Olive, might you stay for tonight's movie?" Lila says.

———

Lila naps while Olive occupies herself with her cell phone and occasionally glances at a cooking show on the television. Vintage movie posters, some autographed, decorate the sitting room walls in Lila's suite, and several framed photographs of Lila's family squeeze between DVDs on ebony media storage shelves. In Lila's bedroom there are three framed black-and-white photographs, all taken inside the Lowe's Valencia Movie Theater. One shows her parents standing at the foot of the theater's grand staircase; another is of Lila leaning into her mother as they sit at the edge of the theater's goldfish pond. The photos show only a slice of the theater's opulent detail. The last photo, which sits on Lila's nightstand next to her bed, is a close-up of her father in the theater's projection booth. As Lila lies down, she glances at the photo. Olive's resemblance to her great-grandfather is uncanny. *So that's why Olive looked familiar.*

Initially, Lila hoped that Olive's visit would be brief; she found their conversation tiresome. But then something changed. Lila felt a kinship with her granddaughter, something she hadn't felt since losing her father. She falls asleep staring at the photograph on her nightstand.

It's a restful nap, no bothersome dreams, and upon waking Lila feels refreshed. She washes her face, applies a bit of lipstick and selects a blue-gray skirt, a midnight blue silk blouse, and silver jewelry. "Now you're the one who's stunning," Olive says.

At dinner, Lila introduces Olive to the others at the table, and Olive charms them with her youth and talk of Julliard.

"Well, I guess the apple doesn't fall far from the tree," one woman says.

Olive admires the woman's brooch. With her chubby fingers, the woman lifts it from the bodice of her dress.

"The masks represent Melpomene and Thalia—the Greek Muses of tragedy and comedy," she says. "I bought it on eBay, especially for Lila's Cinema."

Lila and Olive exchange smiles.

The conversation turns to tonight's movie: *Midnight,* staring Claudette Colbert, Don Ameche, and John Barrymore. All eyes are on Lila and she's a wealth of information, not only about the leading actors, but also about the supporting cast, including Mary Astor and Hedda Hopper, and the screenplay writers, Billy Wilder and Charles Brackett. Lila adds just enough gossip to make it appear as if she were friends or at least acquaintances with these giants of Hollywood's Golden Era, while everyone at the table, including Olive, sits wide-eyed and caught in Lila's spell.

As usual, the parlor is packed, and after Lila shares many of the same details that she just shared with folks at her dinner table, she takes a seat next to Olive. The room goes dark, the movie screen glows, and as *Midnight* scrolls across the large, round face of an ornate clock, Olive takes her grandmother's hand. Lila feels a slight pressure in her chest—possibly a touch of indigestion.

Her thoughts drift to the Valencia Theater. She's nestled between her parents, and her eyes follow the exotic but familiar architectural silhouettes framing the Valencia's auditorium, then she looks up at the canopy of stars, and finally, to the sound of a projector, a movie flashes, bright and inviting.

Lila's father leans in close to her and whispers, *Keep your eyes on the screen, my love, this is the best part.*

Lila squeezes Olive's hand.

The Widower

Disparate and at times desperate, they sit on wood chairs along rectangular tables and stare at computers or cell phones, or through the library's dirty, third-floor windows, across 96th Street at more dirty windows. Some stare with eyes that look inward.

On quiet mornings, they sit alone, each at their own table and lost in their own ruminations, but sometimes they share tables, and sometimes they share demons. Someone mumbles or laughs or yells—apparently at nothing, though nothing is impossible—and the librarian descends from her heavy oak pulpit like a cleric, her finger pressed to her puckered lips.

"You're disturbing the visitors." But she's no exorcist; the only demons she's known are fictional and can be shelved. Sometimes she calls the guard. Sometimes the guard calls the police. That's how demons are expelled from the 96th Street Library, when prose and poetry fail to restrain.

The widower sits alone at his table and checks his email and social media, and then reads articles online in *The New York Times* and *The New Yorker*. His demons are fledgling and mostly controlled, but he feels for those who are more vulnerable to their demons' whims.

Fate is the only difference between the good Samaritan and the stranger, and of credit to neither.

Tall and bone-thin, a man sits at the widower's table. His face is earth-plowed and barren. His hair is a crown of umber mats, streaked with veins of silver. From a torn plastic bag, he lifts a notepad and a thin book of poetry—weathered and dog-eared. With his ebony fingers, he holds the rim and lenses of glasses without arms against his milky eyes. He squints from the poem to his notepad. Carefully, he writes.

The widower glances at the poem—Mary Oliver's "The Bleeding-heart"—and presses his left-thumb against two white-gold wedding bands, one atop the other on his ring finger. They catch the overhead light and quiver in response to the widower's probing thumb.

The bone-thin man traces a line in "The Bleeding-heart." The line reads: *Most things that are important, have you noticed, lack certain neatness.*

Instead of verse, he writes dates and dashes, inscriptions from tombstones—where dashes represent lives, as if a life could be summed up by a dash.

He rocks back and forth; his breathing becomes labored, and he appears agitated. The widower fears that the librarian will call the security guard, and the security guard will call the police. "I met a woman," the widower whispers.

His voice seems to soothe the bone-thin man, whose dark and ashen furrows deepen with anticipation.

"On my way to the library, an old woman called out from her wheelchair. Maybe she was Jesus, or maybe there is no Jesus, and life is a scavenger hunt. She held up a slip of paper with four clues: milk, bananas, rice, and eggs."

The bone-thin man nods and resumes scratching dashes between dates while the widower melds thoughts with whispers. Sometimes it's hard for him to distinguish between what he thinks and says, but with the exception of his ubiquitous sigh, "Whatever," or "What difference does it make?" he mostly contains his thoughts:

...she mumbled and reminded me of my library companions, of the hungry folks in the soup kitchen where I once volunteered, of the residents at the institution where I once worked, of my parents when they were dying, of you when you were dying, and of me when my grief escapes my lips like so much drool.

"She handed me her clues and pointed to a store. I

also pointed, and we mumbled, she in Spanish and I in English, but we understood each other—at least as much as anyone understands another's babble."

He senses the librarian's glare, and presses his finger to his lips as if reminding himself to be silent, but once a memory begins he must follow it to its conclusion, and then wonder if another course of action might have brought about a different end, a better end, or no end at all, but another beginning, or at least a lingering, which is far better than an end—less final, more hopeful.

...the feel of the wheelchair's rubber handles reminded me of you during those final weeks when you no longer had the strength to walk, but then everything reminds me of you.

I pushed her wheelchair into a store too narrow. Girls with plaited and beaded hair stood at cash registers, while boys, short and sturdy, stocked shelves. They stared at the old woman in the wheelchair and at me as if trying to make sense of us.

"They were too young to depend on strangers, kind or otherwise."

The bone-thin man nods and smiles as if acknowledging the Blanche DuBois allusion.

...she called out. A young man handed her two bananas, another a quart of milk. She reached for the rice on her own and pointed to the checkout. I'm not sure why she didn't buy eggs.

"Maybe eggs were no longer important."

The bone-thin man shrugs his shoulders.

...I paid for her food. Outside, I placed the plastic bag into a larger shopping bag that hung from the back of her wheelchair. She held up her hand and stretched out five gnarled, soiled fingers. "Five dolares," she said. I reminded her of the milk, bananas, and rice. "Mañana," she said, but I stopped thinking of tomorrows when the doctor said your cancer had returned, and we lived in the present until even the present became unbearable.

"I don't know how she'll get home or if her milk will spoil in the noon heat."

The bone-thin man looks up from his dashes. His eyes meet the widower's.

"Maybe I shouldn't have left her on the corner, but she wanted to stay, and who was I to tell her she had to leave?"

"Who are you?" the bone-thin man whispers.

The librarian approaches, and the widower fears that he was neither thinking nor whispering; maybe his demons were finally shouting. But it's not his demons she's after. She passes his table and approaches a woman dressed for a blizzard on a summer's day—asleep with her long arms and gloved hands sprawled across a table. The librarian doesn't allow sleeping.

Leave her be, the widower thinks. *Maybe sleep is her only peace.*

The bone-thin man packs up his books, stands, and tightens a frayed belt that cuts across the ridge of his protruding pelvis. Except for the two belt loops, the waist of his baggy pants drapes like a waterfall valance.

...at some point the doctor said we were feeding your cancer, a demon child growing within, cells that wouldn't be aborted and would eventually kill you; I stopped pleading with you to eat.

"Are you hungry?" the widower asks. "I know a place." He packs up his laptop, and the bone-thin man follows him down two flights of stairs. With one hand he clings to his bag of books and with the other he holds the oak railing set above wrought-iron balusters. The widower pauses every few steps to wait and leans against the smooth cool of the marble walls. He's learned to be patient. He's been waiting for two years.

...ever since I told you to go as I lay next to you, and your eyes stared without seeing and your lungs pulsed without breathing. "You're suffering," I said. "I can no longer help you, and I can't bear you suffering." And you listened. While I held you, your chest quivered like a leaf about to surrender, and that was it. Even in death, you were compliant. Now I wait, whether it's on these stairs, or in my bed on sheets as cold and impervious as these mausoleum-like library walls. I wait. Two years have passed, but you're still dead, and I still wait. For what? Who knows?

A year ago, the widower had an epiphany. A woman, small as a child, veiled in soiled worn burlap, lay beneath a streetlight on a busy corner along Fifth Avenue. A stark juxtaposition to the stylish shoppers sashaying in and out of upscale stores. Maybe that's why he stopped.

...like the beggars we saw years ago outside the Vatican. We thought they were staged. "Whatever you do for the least of these, you do for me." Or something like that. But when I spotted the small woman on Fifth Avenue, I paused and searched my pockets. No small bills, so I pressed a twenty into her battered paper cup. No sooner had I turned to walk away, and, "Excuse me, sir. I don't mean to be rude." She held out the twenty. "You might need this someday." I knelt, we spoke, and I assured her that the money was hers, that I had no need for it. Again, I thought of you, and I thought that I will never mean to another what I meant to you. As if you made me real, and without you I'm becoming invisible.

For those brief moments while he knelt on Fifth Avenue he mattered, if only to the woman with the burlap shroud, and she mattered to him. He didn't know her story, but he knew she had one. She didn't suddenly appear on a corner begging for handouts without first being someone's daughter, maybe someone's sibling, or lover, or spouse, or mother, but then something tragic had brought her to this corner, and in part he understood, and he felt that she also understood him, as if she were a clairvoyant who had lifted the twenty-dollar bill from out of the cup and sensed his grief in it. Since then, it's in the company of those who are unseen that he feels most visible, and with whom he's free to grieve without apology.

The widower holds open the door to the Corner Bakery, and the bone-thin man enters, but the cashiers appear surprised to see the widower so late. His routine is to begin his morning at the bakery before he heads to the library, and then after the library to take his dog for a long walk, west to Central Park or east to Carl Schurz Park and along the promenade on the East River. Each morning, when he enters the bakery, one of the cashiers will say, "Your usual?" and he'll nod and extend his morning greeting. He's very fond of the cashiers, especially Nina and Charesse who act as if seeing him has made their day, and unlike his long-time friends and family, they don't expect him to move on with his life, or suggest that it's time for him to meet someone new, or look at him with worried expressions and tell him he's changed.

For those who knew him before, he's no longer one of a pair, but the lone figurine on a shelf; however, it's life that's changed, not him. The cashiers in the Corner Bakery, the folks at the library, the woman sitting in a wheelchair outside the market, the one who was concerned that he might someday need his twenty dollars—not one of them blames him for being alone and lonely. It's not his fault and it's not his responsibility to appease those who feel sorry for him.

Nina's nephew stands beside her at the cash register: short and very thin, with a long mane of dreadlocks that all but cover his narrow bottom, he appears much younger than his twenty years. One morning, the widower extended his usual morning greeting and asked Nina how she was.

"Today not so well. It's the anniversary of my twin sister's death."

"I'm sorry," the widower said. "I understand."

"I know you do," Nina said. A tearful sheen accentuated Nina's warm brown eyes.

"You'll learn to carry the loss, but you'll never forget."

"I don't want to forget." Nina nodded toward the young man standing next to her, just beyond the counter. "She was his mother."

Since then, the widower understands that sometimes Nina's nephew needs to be near his aunt. He rarely speaks. Maybe her smile, her eyes, or a tender glance helps him to remember.

The widower escorts the bone-thin man to one of the small round marble tables along the expansive windowpanes that look out onto Third Avenue.

"Coffee? A bagel? What would you like?" the widower says.

The bone-thin man points to the oversized menus posted above the cashiers, and the widower reads each item aloud until he comes to breakfast sandwiches when the bone-thin man, as if he were about to deliver a sermon, holds up one hand, three fingers curled and his pointer finger and thumb extended. Nina nods.

"One breakfast sandwich," she says.

"And a large coffee," the widower adds.

The bone-thin man thumbs through his book of poetry, and the widower sits next to him without speaking, just thinking and listening to Adele's voice through the bakery's speakers—"Someone Like You."

I'm used to missing you. It's become a part of who I am, as if the missing has replaced the having. I don't understand it, but then there's not much I do understand.

"What difference does it make?"

"It makes a difference."

And the widower stares at the bone-thin man who turns the pages of his book.

"Did you say, 'It makes a difference'?"

The bone-thin man remains silent.

Nina places the sandwich and coffee on the marble table between them, and the bone-thin man empties eight packets of sugar into his coffee.

"I'm going to pay now and leave. I have to walk my dog. Enjoy your meal."

The bone-thin man motions for the widower to wait.

He opens his book of poetry, thumbs through the pages until he comes to "The Bleeding-heart." Carefully, he tears the poem from his book and hands it to the widower.

Back in his small apartment, the widower fastens the poem to the refrigerator with a rainbow magnet. He presses his fingers against the cool paper and remembers when they first saw the apartment.

...a distraction. Better than dwelling on death, and we often spoke of living in Manhattan after you retired. We enjoyed theater, museums, the pulse of the city, and of course Central Park. You talked of volunteering with the Central Park Conservatories. I never thought we'd find something, but when we stepped into this one bedroom on the sixth floor of a prewar low-rise, light flooding the hardwood, parquet floors, and only three blocks from Museum Mile and Central Park, your expression reminded me of the first day I met you, thirty-nine years ago when life was ahead of us. Who was I to remind you that the cancer was terminal? After our purchase offer was accepted, we imagined the walks we'd take, the restaurants we'd dine at, the shows we'd see, and the hours we'd wander through Central Park, under and over stone bridges, around the reservoir and tranquil ponds, listening to music and watching jugglers and other street performers. We spoke of the first snowfall, the first daffodil, the cool escape from summer heat, and autumn color. And though you left before any of that happened, before I even closed on the apartment, we had already imagined those moments. Too many people live without appreciating. In our shared moments of anticipation we appreciated even though we didn't get to live it. They said I was foolish to buy this place, but it was the last thing you wanted. That is aside from wanting what the doctors told us we couldn't have.

"What difference does that all make now?"

His dog cocks his head and looks up at the widower.

"Okay, boy, time for our walk." With leash in hand, the

widower and his dog leave the apartment, take the elevator down six floors to the lobby, step out into the sun, turn left, and then after walking the three blocks to Fifth Avenue, turn right toward Central Park's Conservatory Gardens.

They pass through the majestic Vanderbilt Gate into the six acres of sculpted gardens, and the widower stares, inhales, and transcends the moment. Dashes without dates. Walking the sun-dappled path, under the arc of pink and white crabapple blossoms, he knows that his lips move, and if words escape so be it. Beneath violet wisteria, suspended like a sigh from gnarly bark, he whispers, "Beautiful...I miss you....Look at that cluster of wisteria lit from within," as he points up into the boa of violet flowers, and the dog's amber eyes follow the direction of the widower's finger. The widower laughs and gives the dog's blocky head a rustle. "You think I'm nuts. You may be right."

He sits on a bench beneath a pergola dripping with more wisteria. The dog settles next to the widower's feet. At the far end of the archway a violinist plays Pachelbel's "Canon," and in the Italian-designed center garden circling a geyser fountain, a young couple poses for photographs. The bride's charmeuse, off-the-shoulder dress leaves bare her elegant sable neck and shoulders, which the groom gently kisses.

The widower recalls his wedding. They were no longer young and beautiful like the couple posing before the fountain. It was a practical decision to wed, after the doctor said the cancer was terminal, but it became a joyous celebration nonetheless, where more than a hundred friends and family gathered in their yard under crisscross strands of lights and rainbow streamers, to the sound of guitars and mandolins. It was a celebration of the moment, neither beginning nor end, but a reminder that now is all we really have. Make the most of it. And everyone did. More than a few guests said it was the best wedding they had ever attended.

You rested all afternoon so you could enjoy the evening. And you...we did enjoy ourselves. Who knew when we met that we would someday marry? Several years had passed before we even admitted to friends that we were more than roommates. Those were the tumultuous years following Stonewall. Marches, protests, fighting to either help legislation pass or shut legislation down, caring for dying friends, more struggles, until our biggest challenge. Cancer doesn't discriminate.

Two young men pass where the widower sits. They smile at his dog. They pause before the violinist and take each other's hand. The widower doesn't begrudge them the ease with which they show affection. That's what he and so many others had fought for. Nor does he begrudge the young man and woman posing for wedding photos.

I hope they all have what we had, he thinks, and then

stands to retrace his steps out of the park. Once he brings the dog back to the apartment, he'll go to the gym at the 92nd Street Y, where he'll talk with other old men about frequent nocturnal trips to the bathroom, or listen to one eager little man talk about the women he meets on Match. com. The widower doesn't mention that meeting women on Match.com or anywhere is not one of his priorities. Or maybe, instead of the Y, he'll take the Q to the West Side and catch a foreign film at Lincoln Plaza.

His cell phone rings, and he knows where this conversation is going when his friend says, "Not sure if this is appropriate or if you'd be interested, but…" His friend proceeds to explain that she's in a reading group, and there's this lovely man, divorced, and he recently came out.

"Soft spoken, very sweet, in fact he reminds me of… well, you know. I don't know if you're ready. But maybe next time you drive up from the city, I can have a little dinner party. Who knows? He's never been in a relationship with a man, and says that he hopes there's still time for him to meet someone special. You're special."

The widower explains that he doesn't think it would be a good idea; however, he thanks her for caring. Later he sends her an email and addresses it *Dear Shadchen* (matchmaker in Yiddish) to make light of the subject. He doesn't want her to feel bad for trying. Again, he thanks her for caring.

Sleep no longer comes easily. It's usually one or two, or later before he shuts down his computer or closes his book and tries to sleep, a sleep that is frequently interrupted by urges to pee or a need to turn from one side to the other.

…but they're solitary turns, no longer my chest pressed against your back, then yours pressed against mine. You once said this was your favorite time of day, just the two of us like two spoons wrapped in cool sheets, blankets, and darkness, as if everything else had vanished, but then you vanished, and only the sheets, blankets, and darkness remain.

"Your usual?" Nina says.

"Yes, thank you, and how are you this morning?"

"I'm well, thank you."

"I see your granddaughter has been painting your fingernails again," the widower says.

Nina fans out her fingers like two shimmering deltas. Her fingernails glitter gold and silver. "Yes, not my style, but she has fun doing it. By the way, your friend seemed to enjoy his lunch yesterday."

"My friend?" Then the widower remembers the bone-thin man, and he wonders if he'll see him at the library, but there is no bone-thin man or anyone else to join him as he sits alone at the table at the 96th Street Library and opens his laptop to check his email, social media, and then read articles online in *The New York Times* and *The New Yorker*.

What Took You So Long?

Nick said that the will granted Ida lifetime rights to the house and its surrounding eight acres. Nothing would be sold as long as she lived there. He also mentioned that he was the sole heir and was quite comfortable with his Aunt Winifred's wishes. Ida asked him if he wanted a drink.

"Beer or something stronger?" Ida said. A lit cigarette hung from her downturned mouth, and its blue smoke blurred the February frost of her features—abrupt angles and sharp edges as if years had eroded all softness. Photos showed a younger, handsome Ida, but never a pretty Ida. And before Ida, photos of Millie framed Winifred's mirror, but Nick never met Millie—nor Ida for that matter, not until the day he told her the details of his aunt's will. As if she hadn't already known them. They sat beside a creek, beneath hemlocks, and she used gardening shears to cut open the plastic bag of powdered ash and chips of bone.

"Here, you do the rest," Ida said, and handed him the open bag, then lit another cigarette.

"Isn't there something we should say?" Nick asked. "Maybe read a favorite poem or prayer?"

"I've already said good-bye," Ida muttered. "This isn't Freddie. No way she'd be sealed in a bag. How's that for a prayer?" Maybe the cigarette smoke caused Ida's eyes to tear. Nick whispered Amen.

He thinks back to that day and tastes the shock of Ida's Bloody Marys, more vodka and hot sauce than tomato juice. He unfolds a letter signed by Jonathan Wheaton, Esq., Skaneateles, New York, and then reads Ida's enclosed obituary, which says nothing of Winifred, just as Winifred's obituary said nothing of Ida. An empty obituary, as empty as the words he and Ida shared that day under the hemlocks.

Now the house belongs to Nick, to do with as he pleases. Only his. No kids to consider and, as of four months ago, no wife either. An amicable divorce, little fuss over money. She made more than him anyway. No pets. She claimed dogs and cats made her wheeze. Plants? Who had time to water them? She found time for affairs, though. He pretended not to notice, like he pretended not to notice the birth control pills she said she stopped taking after he suggested children—only a suggestion, he wasn't one to make demands. But his wife's indiscretion with a delivery boy, one of Nick's high school students, shredded Nick's capacity to deny. When he asked her for a divorce, she simply smiled and said, "What took you so long?"

He folds Ida's obituary and considers the time and effort required to sell his aunt's house, a much-needed distraction. He remembers little of the house except, as with many old farmhouses, its state of quaint decline, and the 1950s flea-market furnishings. No heirlooms to discover among the laminate and Naugahyde, but the surrounding trees were magnificent, and it was only four hours from the George Washington Bridge. A change of scenery would do him good before starting his new teaching position in the fall.

———

As Nick pulls into the driveway—his Accord's tires crunching the crushed-stone driveway—a forest of conifers and deciduous trees give way to threesomes, couples, and solitary specimens framing the house. Maybe he inherited his love of trees from his aunt, but other than random facts, Nick knows little of his Aunt Winifred. His father's only sibling, ten years his father's senior, she served in the Women's Army Corps in World War II, graduated from Wells College, worked as a school social worker, hated the name Winifred, owned a house upstate, and had a *friend*, Ida, whose very name caused Nick's mother to roll her eyes. He had been in Winifred's company at family gatherings—holidays, graduations, weddings, funerals, etc.—but Nick found her to be aloof, or, as his mother said, cold.

Nick's paternal grandparents boasted white Protestant stock dating back to Mayflower times, but Nick had grown up mostly around his maternal relatives—Sicilians and other Italians, a stark contrast to his father's family. Nick's paternal grandparents and aunt felt that his father had married down; in fact, they didn't even attend the wedding. When Nick's father died prematurely, Nick's mother—not one to forgive, even after Nick's grandparents spent years trying to make amends—said, "Your father's death is a curse from his heartless parents."

Nick's mother often complained to his father, "You know damn well that if Winifred had found a husband and given your parents grandchildren, we'd never hear from them." No mention of why Winifred didn't find a husband, just more eye-rolling. And Nick's grandparents, already tight-lipped, never mentioned Winifred's personal life. Only the few photographs circling the mirror in Winifred's childhood bedroom in her parents' house—where she slept when she visited, and then moved back into during her parents' declining years— hinted of Winifred's relationships.

"Who's that, Aunt Winifred?" a very young Nick had asked as he pointed to the photo.

"Ida," she answered.

"And that, Aunt Winifred?"

"Millie," she answered.

But no matter how many times Nick asked her, she offered the same terse response. He learned early not to ask her questions.

From the front porch he looks out across Willowdale Road, where acres of hayed land slope away to hedgerows of willows, sugar maples, and ash trees. He views glimmers of Otisco Lake through breaks in the hedgerows, and beyond the lake, wooded hills frame patches of farmland. Above the hills, blue-white clouds, like immense vaporous circus animals, lumber across the sky and cast giant shadows along the landscape.

Inside, the house smells of shut windows and loneliness. Less-faded patches of wood flooring, carpet, and wallpaper speak of missing furniture. The lawyer assured Nick that Ida's nieces removed only *their* aunt's belongings, probably to furnish a great niece or nephew's college apartment. Who else would want such junk? One room is empty, except for a photograph of his aunt—possibly Ida's bedroom, or a study. Numerous framed photographs hang on walls or perch on a dresser in a fully furnished bedroom, most likely Winifred's. As in her childhood bedroom, pictures are taped around a mirror.

He recognizes his grandparents and Ida and maybe

Millie. But there are also many photos of unfamiliar people. Snapshots of Winifred's life: picnics, boating, fishing, and cross-country skiing. A studio portrait of Winifred and Ida resembling each other the way old couples often do sits at the corner of a large oak desk next to a small framed snapshot Winifred must have taken of Nick at his college graduation. He lifts the picture and examines it, surprised to find his image among his aunt's pictorial archives.

He unpacks the few things he brought with him and places them in the dresser—shirts, underwear, and socks atop of his aunt's clothes—then hangs a pair of jeans and a rain jacket in the closet. He hears:

"Hello! Anyone here? Hello!"

Nick closes the closet door, walks out of Winifred's bedroom and down the steep, creaking steps back to the living room. The front door is ajar, and a man leans into the house, his feet remaining planted on the porch.

"You Nick? Freddie's nephew?"

"Yes," Nick answers. He remembers that Ida called his aunt Freddie.

"I'm Merrill. Been keepin' an eye on this place since Ida went to the hospital. I figured you'd show up sooner or later."

Merrill's about the same age as Nick (50ish), and despite the lines in his tanned skin, especially bracketing his smile, and his hair thinning at the crown, Merrill reminds

Nick of his students. Maybe it's Merrill's wiry build, or the way his T-shirt is half tucked into his grass-stained jeans, or the way he looks Nick right in the eyes, as if he hasn't yet learned not to trust.

"I received a letter and the obituary from the lawyer," Nick says.

Merrill shakes his head. "Yeah, lung cancer. Ida smoked like a chimney. Lousy way to go. She stayed here almost to the end. She was a tough one. Mind if I come in? Holdin' this door open, I'm invitin' flies."

"No…I mean, sure, I don't mind. I just got here myself."

Merrill kicks off his shoes and lets the screen door slam behind him. The big toe of his right foot peeks through a hole in his sock, and there's black under his fingernails. Nick wonders if Merrill works one of the local farms.

"Sorry I can't offer you a beer or something, but please sit down." Nick looks around the room. "Guess that's easier said than done. Not much to sit on."

"You sit there," Merrill says. He points to a well-worn recliner and raises his voice as he disappears through an open door. "I'll get a chair from the kitchen." Merrill walks back into the living room carrying a chrome kitchen chair with a gray and red vinyl back and seat. Much of the vinyl is cracked. "Yeah, I saw one of Ida's nieces an' some kids load up a U-Haul. A couple of her nieces used to visit once in a while, more so as Ida got sicker. Guess they just about emptied the place."

The men sit facing each other. Nick's creased jeans and Burberry T-shirt speak of Manhattan, a stroll through Central Park and a beer at Tavern on the Green; Merrill's jeans and T-shirt speak of jeans and a T-shirt.

"You're lucky they left that." Merrill points to an oil painting: sharp contrasts between dark and light, an arc of boughs, a bracken of ferns, rocks and fallen trees interrupting the rush of water, splashes of light against dark browns and greens—a spring representation of the November creek where Nick and Ida had left Winifred's ashes.

Nick examines the painting. "I recognize that spot."

"Their favorite," Merrill says.

"Their?"

"Freddie an' Ida. They loved it. The creek runs along the west side of the land, borderin' what used to be the Sharps' place. In summer Freddie an' Ida sat there before dinner an' had their drinks. Cocktails, they called 'em. We had plenty of picnics by that creek—Freddie an' Ida, the Sharps, an' me an' Victor, an' sometimes musician friends come visit for most of the summer. I don't know how they managed in this little house, but they did. Those were good times. Once, one of your aunt's dogs—you know she always had those corgis, looked like God forgot to give them legs—well, it came nose-to-nose with a tiny fawn that was all curled up in the tall weeds. There they was, just starin' at each other, tryin' to figure things out while we was drinkin' our cocktails. Freddie grabbed the dog's collar an' the fawn stood up on its skinny legs an' wobbled up into the woods callin' its mama. Freddie loved nature. She knew the name of every kind of tree an' wildflower. Like one of those guide books."

"Sounds as if you knew my aunt well."

"'Bout as well as a person can know another. Real nice lady. Funny. Ida wasn't so funny, but still nice. Anyways, it's a good thing Ida's niece left that painting. Victor's stuff always sold pretty good but got pricier after he died. I'd say you could get a couple of grand for that one. Funny how what folks do is better appreciated after they're gone.

"Anyways, I just stopped by to introduce myself. You know, in case you need somethin'. You're probably gonna sell, but you should do a little paintin' or fixin' first, so you get a better price. The house ain't much, but the land's pretty. I helped plant a lot of the trees, back when I was a boy." Merrill stands and extends his right hand. "Real nice meetin' you. I'm pretty good at fixin' stuff. You need anythin', I live right down the road. The old Victorian at the four corners, across from the schoolhouse. Just turn right, out of your driveway. Less than a mile."

Victorian, not a dilapidated farmhouse or trailer, Nick thinks. *Guess I had that wrong.*

At some point during his teen years, Nick assumed

that his aunt was a lesbian, but he didn't give it much thought. His father's family was reclusive—Winifred just a little more so. But as he sits on the front porch listening to the trill of tree frogs and the drum of a bull frog, he imagines his aunt's life here with Ida—a full, rich life, beyond rolling eyes and snide remarks. Maybe Winifred and Ida had been lovers or maybe the weight of oppressive times confined them to their separate bedrooms. Regardless, they were a couple and from the little Merrill said it appears as if they were happy—happier than Nick had been in his marriage, that much was certain.

Above dark, undulating hills the sky is awash in pink and orange. Nick picks at his macaroni and cheese, a box mix he found in the cupboard. What might it be like to live here? Merrill had mentioned that across from his house is a school, though Nick can't imagine a school located in such a remote area—although he also can't imagine Merrill living in a Victorian house. Soon, Nick would begin teaching at a new school—why not make a big change? The thought of a new life away from rolling eyes and snide remarks appeals to Nick. He leans against the porch railing and takes in the silhouettes of trees and of bats feasting on insects. Not Manhattan, but is that so bad?

Hours later, an owl's mantra lulls him through his open bedroom window. Wasn't Merrill too young and, considering Winifred's snobbery, too illiterate to have

215

been her friend? And what was the artist's name—Victor? Nick's glad that Ida's niece left the painting and glad that Merrill visited. It's been years since Nick's felt glad about anything. He draws the frayed quilt up over his shoulder and sleeps an unbroken sleep, more peaceful than he's slept in a very long time.

The next morning, fog obscures Otisco Lake, but by the time Nick showers and shaves and slips on his jeans and a fresh T-shirt, then gets in his car and takes a left onto Willowdale, the fog has lifted. He retraces yesterday's drive past farmhouses, some in the same disrepair as his aunt's or worse, some restored. He also passes trailers and an eclectic mix of new homes, modest doublewides and large contemporaries with expansive windows. A dairy farm to Nick's right appears abandoned except for cows grazing in a pasture, peeking out of dilapidated barns, or standing alongside the road as if waiting for a bus. The farmhouse and barns, overgrown with sumac and grapevine, lean precariously. Feral cats vanish like wizards into clumps of chicory and Queen Anne's lace.

The GPS advises Nick to turn left, and he meanders upward through cornfields that soak up morning sun, wisps of fog clinging to their silk like languid spirits; a flock of wild turkeys awkwardly take flight. When he comes to Route 41, he turns right onto the crest of the hill between Otisco and Skaneateles Lakes, toward the village of Skaneateles. To his left a pull-out overlooks the expanse of Skaneateles Lake, more elegant than Otisco, and it glitters under the morning sun as if boasting of its splendor. The road descends, Skaneateles Lake appears to his left, and within ten minutes he arrives in the village, where stately homes lounge on expansive lawns accessorized with hydrangea and hibiscus and framed in ornate wrought iron. Gradually, these mini-estates morph into commercial buildings—on the lakeside is a stretch of two-story brick buildings, with first-floor shops and second-floor condos.

Nick parks his car, buys a coffee and scone in one of the village shops, finds a bench in the lakeside park with a stunning view of sailboats and Gatsbycsque estates, and he savors his coffee and scone, and the peaceful tranquility of this picturesque village. Folks stroll the promenade between Nick and the lake, and Nick spots an elderly couple returning arm-in-arm from a walk on the pier.

Had Winifred and Ida enjoyed this lakeside paradise, exchanged greetings with the locals, nodded at tourists? He can't imagine Merrill in this village, but then Merrill is an enigma, with his stories of sipping cocktails, and his grimy fingernails, holey socks, and homey vernacular. Again Nick wonders about the artist—Victor? Merrill had said, "me and Victor." Did he mean as a couple? Nick shrugs and tosses the last few crumbs of his scone to some tenacious ducks.

Nick scans the listings in a real estate office window. The hefty prices—not just for lakeside mansions, but also for smaller, more modest homes throughout the village—are quite impressive. He enters the office and learns that Skaneateles prices are an anomaly and that homes surrounding Otisco Lake sell for much less. The realtor tells him that for the most part, buyers from New York City are amazed by the bargains they find in Central New York.

"Of course that's good news for the buyer, not the seller," she chuckles. She hands Nick her card. "But I'm sure that I could get you a good price. You said the house has a view of the lake? Otisco is one of the Finger Lakes' best-kept secrets. Just lovely."

He pockets the agent's card, thanks her, inquires about a supermarket, and then makes his way back to his car. After grocery shopping, he tours the village side streets, and admires the modest but pristine homes with the hefty price tags. He passes Skaneateles High School and remembers that before last year, he had loved teaching.

That afternoon, Nick walks down his driveway to Willowdale Road and turns right, in search of Merrill's Victorian—an image he still can't wrap his head around. While walking past dense woodland, two log cabins, and a trailer, he pictures Merrill's house to be a modest but equally dilapidated version of Bates Mansion, until a tail wagging, scruffy white dog distracts him.

"Hey, boy!" Nick bends to pet the dog, and then Nick spots, to his left, an old one-room schoolhouse with a belfry and a fresh coat of white paint, under a canopy of sugar maples. *So this is the school Merrill mentioned*, Nick thinks. And beyond the trees, to Nick's right and across the road from the school, stands a Victorian house, just as Merrill said, but not at all what Nick imagined—high-gabled, draped in gingerbread, and freshly painted like the schoolhouse, but with multiple colors. Resplendent gardens border the foundation, and the lawn looks more like carpet than grass. Slack-jawed, Nick approaches the house, and the white dog barks as if announcing Nick. Merrill appears from out of a small barn as impeccable as the house.

"Hey, Hobo, you brought a visitor." Merrill holds a wrench. He runs his right forearm across his face, smearing grease or soil on his left cheek and smiles. "Just let me clean up," Merrill says then disappears back into the barn.

Nick examines the house. Every detail is perfect, as if it were built yesterday.

"You like these kinds of houses?" Merrill startles Nick. His hair is wet and freshly combed, and he smells of soap.

"There's a place, a short ferry ride from Sag Harbor— Long Island," Nick says. "We used to vacation there when we were first…I mean, I used to go there years ago. There were a lot of houses like this, though most of them were much smaller than this one."

"This one's Queen Anne." Merrill folds his calloused hands behind his back and nods his scruffy chin as if lecturing. "But all that fancy stuff is called Eastlake, after Charles Eastlake."

Nick stares at him incredulously. Who is this man? Again, Merrill reminds Nick of his students, attempting to impress the teacher, but so unguarded and innocent. Though innocent might not be the right word for high school boys, considering that a twelfth grader in Nick's American Literature class copulated with Nick's wife, then boasted of his conquest to every student in the small private high school.

"It was built by a Methodist minister, hoping to build more an' turn his land into some kind of religious camp. Not sure why it didn't work out, but there's all kinds of stories. Mostly idle gossip. You know how small-minded folks can be." Merrill punctuates his commentary with a nod and a broad smile. "Wanna' go inside?"

Before Nick has a chance to answer, Merrill's on the porch, removing his shoes and holding the screen door open for Nick. Nick follows him then bends to remove his own shoes. "No need. Mine's always dirty, but you look like you just stepped out of a magazine." Nick blushes, something he has no recollection of ever having done before.

The interior accents are even more pristine than the exterior: high-gloss hardwood floors and wainscoting, coved arches at the juncture of walls and ceilings, an entry hall staircase with ornate, fluted newel posts and balusters. The two parlors and dining room are replete with European antiques, intricately carved and heavily lacquered; the upholstery is plush and of warm, subdued golds and greens and burgundies, as are the drapes, which hang from heavy rods trimmed with gilded finials. On the walls are tapestries and oils, similar to the lone painting in Nick's sparse living room.

"Yes, Victor did those," Merrill says as Nick observes the paintings.

"This place is amazing," Nick doesn't add what he's thinking. *Are you sure that you live here?*

"An' a bear to clean, just ask Violet," Merrill says.

"Violet?"

"Yeah, she's the one who keeps this place so spotless. I take care of the outside an' Violet takes care of the inside. Used to be my Granma who done the cleaning an' most of the cooking." Merrill lifts a silver framed photograph from a fringed scarf covering a grand piano and hands it to Nick. "That's Granma an me."

A sepia Merrill, about twelve years old, folds himself into the pleats of an old woman's apron. They stand next to lilacs in full bloom. Nick returns the photo to the piano, eyes other photos of Merrill at various ages, and pauses at one of Merrill with an older man. The man is tall, slender, and formal in his dress and posture.

221

"That's me an' Victor," Merrill says. "He'd fasten the camera to a tripod, have us pose, then he'd set something on the camera, then run back next to me an' the camera would shoot the picture. I was never much of a photographer. Victor always took the pictures. Guess it was the artist in him. I'll show you upstairs, then we'll get somethin' to drink."

The second-floor furnishings are as opulent as the first floor's. From the master bedroom, Merrill opens a small-paned French door to a tea porch, and—once back in the hallway—they look into smaller bedrooms, then pass a door Merrill doesn't open. He mentions that it's to Victor's studio.

The kitchen is bright and more functional than decorative. An old farmer drives a honey wagon down Willowdale Road, and a whiff of aged manure drifts through the screen door and open kitchen windows. Hobo sniffs at the air and Merrill points to a room off the kitchen. "That's my room," Merrill says. The stack of books on a nightstand surprise Nick.

"Lemonade?" Merrill asks.

They sit at a small kitchen table and Nick speaks of his conversation with the Skaneateles realtor.

Merrill chuckles. "Yeah, some maps of the Finger Lakes don't even show Otisco…like it's a bastard kid. May be one of the runts, but if you ask me it's the prettiest lake, especially the southwest part, right below us. Tomorrow we can drive down to the lake in the gator."

"I'd like that," Nick says, though he has no idea what a gator is.

The worst part of Nick's wife having had sex with his student was how people treated him differently afterward. Students averted their eyes and giggled, and faculty avoided conversations that went beyond discussing the weather. Nick's mother summed it up with, "Well, it's late, but finally you're rid of that bitch."

Merrill doesn't know about any of this; instead, he rambles on about how his family has lived in this area forever, and his great grandfather then his grandfather owned a boat livery on the east side of Otisco, until his grandfather drowned when he got tangled up in his fishing line. After the family lost the livery, his grandma went to work for Victor. And all the while Merrill talks, he looks right at Nick, with no pity in his eyes, and Nick enjoys the refreshing company of this unassuming man.

After a deep breath and a swallow of lemonade, Merrill asks, "So when do you think you'll sell?"

"I don't know. Maybe I won't sell. Maybe they can use an English teacher in Skaneateles."

Merrill laughs. "Now wouldn't that be somethin'."

"I'm just thinking aloud."

"Well, you keep thinkin' that way. With Ida gone, seems like all folks do is leave here."

"Do you miss her?" Nick's surprised by his own words. He's not one to question. "Sorry, I didn't mean to pry."

"That's okay. I miss all of them. Guess that's the problem with havin' friends that are old. They up an' die on you, or they move to Florida. That's what the Sharps did... the couple that lived on the other side of the creek from Freddie an' Ida. It's like, I'm also old, but I'm not near dyin' and I don't think I'd like Florida." Merrill chuckles.

Nick doesn't think of Merrill as old. If anything, he seems to Nick like one of Peter Pan's Lost Boys, and earlier, when Nick viewed the photograph of a young Merrill with the tall, slender, and much older Victor, he got a queasy feeling, but Nick is a pro at dismissing feelings, queasy or otherwise.

The following morning, while the sun still shines on the west side of Otisco Lake, before it disappears behind the heavily treed shoreline, Merrill drives the gator, which resembles a heavy-duty golf cart, down the steep, rutted, winding road, past ravines and abrupt drop-offs.

Merrill points to water trickling down a glossy crag and explains to Nick that in spring those trickles are a roaring waterfall and the woods are filled with wildflowers.

"Freddie, Ida, and Victor had strong opinions about their favorite flowers," Merrill says, and Nick stares at Merrill's profile as he drives and reminisces aloud. "Freddie was partial to trillium, Ida loved bloodroot, but Victor said Jack in the Pulpit were the most dignified, with little Jack standing erect in its fold of leaves. I didn't have any particular preference. I just liked that it was spring and the woods came back to life." Merrill shrugs his shoulders. "Too bad people aren't like the woods."

Nick thinks to place his hand on Merrill's shoulder or even take Merrill's hand, to extend some physical show of comfort, but of course he doesn't.

Merrill parks the gator, and they follow a steep path, traversing a carpet of ferns and myrtle. Exposed tree roots anchor a bank that might otherwise give way to a sylvan landslide. They pass the remnants of a stone fireplace and chimney, and then a shed, and finally, along the shale shoreline, a rowboat with a small outboard motor sits next to two kayaks propped on their sides, leaning onto each other as if for support.

"Been a dry summer," Merrill says, "Lake hasn't been this low since '96."

The lake mirrors the blue sky, and the shadows of gulls and a great blue heron. Merrill opens the shed door and removes two life jackets and paddles. He slips one of the jackets over his T-shirt with its image of a folksy trio and the words Happiness is an Otisco Firehouse Pancake, then hands Nick the other jacket and a pair of water shoes. "Zebra mussels. You'll cut up your feet."

He points to the two kayaks. "Those were Freddie an'

Ida's. Ida gave them to me after Freddie died, but I was just watchin' them. Kind of like I was watchin' the house. They're yours now. Do you like kayaking?"

"Never tried it," Nick says.

"Well it's a good day to learn."

After a brief lesson on getting in and paddling, Nick's kayak glides easily behind Merrill's. They hug the west shore of the lake, craggy and dense with hemlock, hornbeam, beech, basswood, ash, and aspen whose leaves flutter like the wings of a thousand silver butterflies. A regal sycamore dwarfs the other trees.

"Another plus for Otisco over Skaneateles," Merrill shouts.

"What's that?"

"Weekdays there ain't much traffic on the lake. Come fall, it's even quieter."

Nick scans the lake. Merrill is right; there are more gulls and ducks than people. A largemouth bass breaks the water's surface.

Merrill waits for Nick to catch up. "On Skaneateles, all those folks with the fancy houses have to show off their fancy boats. It's like a damn pissin' contest. Sometimes Freddie an' Ida would drive their kayaks over the hill to Skaneateles, an' after they come back from fighting the wakes of those big, fancy power boats, Ida would complain about wastin' the day, an' Freddie would say somethin' about the grass being greener. They liked bickerin'.

Seemed like they just liked talkin' to each other." Nick finds it difficult to imagine his aunt being a talker, considering how quiet it was in his grandparents' house, even when his aunt was there.

"Unfortunately, I didn't know my aunt very well," Nick says.

Both men stop paddling. Merrill holds onto the rim of Nick's kayak, and they drift into a bog of milfoil. Nick looks into the weeds and thinks of the books on Merrill's nightstand and asks, "How long did you know Freddie?" This is the first time he calls his aunt Freddie and the first time he notices Merrill's eyes look inward.

"When Granma's cancer got bad, we moved in with Victor; he was already good friends with Freddie an' Ida. I was about twelve. They helped me an' Victor take care of Granma, especially the personal stuff."

"I'm sorry," Nick says.

"'Bout what? Old folks die. It's only natural."

—————

Before the school year begins, Nick resigns from his new position at a public high school in Manhattan and sublets his studio apartment. Neither Skaneateles nor the other surrounding high schools are hiring. His best offer is a tentative yes as a long-term sub, to replace a teacher going on maternity leave come Janurary in Homer, about 20 miles south. Violet, Merrill's housekeeper and, as it turns out, his cousin, had suggested that Nick apply at Homer High—her daughter being the pregnant English teacher.

Given the exceptionally warm and dry September days, Merrill and Nick scrape and paint the outside of Nick's house. The men share an easy rapport and, without asking, Nick learns more about Freddie and Ida—stories about Freddie's job as a school social worker, Ida teaching music at a small college, vacations in the Adirondacks and on Cape Cod, and about their many friends and how much they loved to entertain. Merrill speaks of musician friends visiting all summer; of summer nights filled with music, laughter, fireflies, and, of course, cocktails; and Nick misses this aunt that he never really knew. Merrill doesn't say more about his grandmother being sick or about when they moved in with Victor, and Nick doesn't ask—not that he doesn't have questions. Like, why had Merrill come to live with his grandmother? And why had he stayed with Victor after his grandmother died? And who was this Victor anyway? Nick leaves these questions in the bog of milfoil.

———

The cottage-red clapboards with forest green trim complement the changing leaves, and though a few details need a second coat, the evenings turn too cool for the paint to set. Merrill suggests a drive to the apple orchards. He'll show Nick where he's worked on-and-off since he was a kid—pruning trees, harvesting apples, and pressing cider.

"When you're ready, give a call," Merrill says. "We'll go in my pickup."

Instead of calling, Nick walks to Merrill's house. The truck is in the driveway, but there's no sign of Merrill or Hobo. During the past month and a half, Nick has visited Merrill enough times to feel comfortable entering the house unannounced, so he opens the kitchen door and calls Merrill's name, but there's no answer. He passes an empty coffee cup on the kitchen table, calls into the living room, and then stands at the foot of the staircase to the second floor and calls again.

Nick barely hears Merrill's response. "In the attic. Come on up."

Nick climbs the stairs to the second floor. "Which way?" he shouts at the ceiling. "Through the closet in the master bedroom," Merrill answers.

The first door Nick opens is to the bathroom, and the second is to a room he doesn't recognize, but he remembers his first time in the house, when Merrill mentioned something about Victor's studio, and in the dark he can barely see silhouettes of large canvases, probably on easels, and more canvases propped against walls. He opens the door further, and the canvases appear to be covered with heavy fabric, maybe tapestries.

"Did you find the stairs?"

Nick leaves the studio and closes the door behind him. He finds the closet door in the master bedroom ajar and climbs the stairs to the attic.

"There you are," Merrill says. "I thought you got lost." A naked light bulb barely illuminates Merrill's back. He's hunched over in a corner beneath the roof's steep pitch, holding a flashlight. "From outside, I noticed a few holes in the eaves. Carpenter bees. With the heavy frosts, they're gone now. Just checkin' under this insulation to see if they drilled their way into the attic."

Nick hears the words *bees* and *insulation*, but his thoughts are on Victor's studio, and while he and Merrill drive to the orchards, pick apples, and buy cider, his thoughts linger there in the dark studio, surrounded by the curious silhouettes. Several times Merrill asks if Nick is troubled by something, and each time Nick answers no. After all, why should Nick care so much about those veiled canvases, or Victor, for that matter? For someone who has long made a practice of not asking questions, now all Nick has are questions.

Before leaving the orchard, one of the owners complains to Merrill about being short staffed, and Merrill agrees to work for a few days. He asks Nick to join him. "We can use a break from painting."

Come Monday, Nick feigns a stomach bug. He knows

that while Merrill works at the orchard, the house will be unlocked, and he'll have the opportunity to more closely investigate Victor's studio. Since stumbling upon the veiled canvases, Nick—already concerned that Victor may have molested the boy Merrill—is now obsessed, and he hopes to find answers in Victor's studio.

Nick enters the house through the unlatched kitchen screen door, but finds the studio locked. He goes back downstairs, and searches the kitchen and Merrill's bedroom for a key.

Aside from books stacked on Merrill's nightstand, there's also a wall of bookshelves, and among how-to books are works of fiction, including classics by Wilde, Forster, and Mann. Nick lifts a copy of *Death In Venice* and a newspaper article spills out.

LOCAL ARTIST DIES IN FIRE

Victor Carpenter succumbed to smoke inhalation. Upon seeing smoke, boaters came ashore, to find Carpenter facedown outside of his burning camp. By the time fireboats arrived, the Otisco Lake camp was engulfed. Arson is suspected….

Nick sits at the edge of Merrill's bed and skims the rest of the article. At the time of the fire, Merrill, referred to as Carpenter's handyman, was repairing a barn on Willowdale Road. Nick sighs, returns the article to the book, slides open the drawer to the nightstand, and discovers a key ring with a single key. His stomach feels queasy, and his own breaths startle him. He lifts the key and closes the drawer.

Upon entering the studio and opening the drapes, light pours onto dust-covered tubes of dry paint, brushes, palettes, and canvases leaning against walls; tapestries cover four canvases propped on easels. A thick layer of dust obscures unfinished paintings of scenery, cursory portraits, and sketches of nudes. Fearful that Merrill might soon return, Nick peels away one tapestry, another, and then another. Three paintings of the young Merrill, partially nude and in classic poses: Pan, the god of the wild, with the hindquarters, legs, and horns of a goat; Ganymede being abducted by Zeus in the form of an eagle; Narcissus mesmerized by his own reflection.

Nick recalls viewing an exhibit of Baron Wilhelm von Gloeden's photography in Taormina, Sicily—sepia photographs of nude Sicilian boys, peasant youth with dirty fingernails and dirty feet in classic poses before the backdrop of ancient ruins and Sicily's unforgiving landscape. He remembers his mother rolling her eyes when speaking of Winifred, and he also thinks of the first day he met Merrill and of Merrill's dirty fingernails and his toe poking through a hole in his sock.

Merrill is a man. But he wasn't always. Not when he posed for these paintings.

Arson is suspected. That's what the article said, and now Nick fears—even more than he had—that Merrill might have been the victim of the pedophile Victor until he finally took his revenge. But hadn't Nick's high-school student bragged of fucking Nick's wife? Maybe Merrill was the seducer, for attention or money or as a joke. *Not Merrill*, Nick thinks, and he's suddenly weary of rolling eyes, smirks, and secrets.

One canvas remains covered, and as Nick removes the final tapestry, he knows why he cares so much about the other paintings and their implications. He knows why he gave up his job, subletted his apartment, and moved into a house that was all but falling down. Nick views the painting, of the adult Merrill wearing a T-shirt, jeans, and sneakers and staring back at him with his candid and endearing expression.

For the past month and a half, Nick's been happier than he's ever been. "What took you so long?" Wasn't that the question his wife had asked him?

Nick hears the front door close. He doesn't cover the paintings or draw the drapes, nor does he lock the studio door. In the living room, Violet untangles the vacuum cleaner cord. Nick startles her.

"I thought you boys were working at the orchards," she

says. Violet is at most ten years older than Nick, but to her all men are boys.

Nick sits on the steps. He's at eye level with Violet. "May I ask you a question, Violet?" Just considering asking the question feels liberating to Nick. He's been in Violet's company a half dozen times and likes her no-nonsense ways, but he's not sure if he can trust her. It doesn't matter. Later, he plans to ask Merrill the same question.

"Sure," Violet says. She plugs in the vacuum.

"Did Victor hurt Merrill?"

Violet looks at the key ring and key dangling from Nick's finger, then looks Nick in the eyes with the same forthright expression as Merrill's. "Honey, that boy was hurt long before he ever met Victor. If anything, Victor saved him."

Nick tries to object, but Violet holds up her long fingers, as if stopping traffic. "I don't know what you think you just seen, but when Merrill came to live with our grandma, he had stopped talking. Who knows which one of his mama's no-good boyfriends had stolen his voice or what else they took from him." Violet purses her lips as if she's about to spit. "When Grandma got sick, Victor took them both in. No one else would have done that. My mama was working full-time, and I was also working and pregnant with my first baby, and my uncles lived far away, and Merrill's mama wasn't worth the time of day.

"After Grandma died, you couldn't pry Merrill away

from Victor. Why would you want to? Even after Victor was gone, he took care of that boy. He left enough money to keep Merrill in this house and to keep me cleaning it. Didn't Freddie ever tell you how Victor helped that boy? Now I got to start vacuuming or I'll never get my work done."

Violet presses the toe of her shoe against the vacuum switch, and Nick walks back upstairs. He draws the drapes and covers the paintings, then locks the door to Victor's studio. As he passes Violet on his way to Merrill's bedroom, she turns off the vacuum. "I take it you know where that key belongs," she says.

That evening, Nick sits on his porch. The air smells of wood smoke, and the moon is so bright Nick can barely see the stars. Hobo barks and Nick spots Merrill and Hobo approaching. Nick wonders if their glow comes from the moon or from something within them.

Merrill waves a half-gallon jug: "Fresh cider!" In his other hand there appears to be a fiddle.

"Time for cocktails!" Merrill shouts.

Who is this man? Nick thinks, and he can't help but smile.

Acknowledgments

2012, *Grave Companions*, Nimrod International Journal of Prose and Poetry

2012, *Forgiveness*, Off The Rocks, Volume 16

2013, *What Took You So Long*, Saints and Sinners: New Fiction From The Festival, runner-up

2013, *What Took You So Long*, Nimrod International Journal of Prose and Poetry

2013, *Oxford Avenue Station*, Gertrude Press, Volume 19

2013, *Touching The Elephant*, North American Review, Volume 298, Number 1

2013, *Fragile Moments* (titled Small Wisdoms), North American Review, Volume 298, Number 4

2016, *Emma's*, Saints and Sinners: New Fiction From The Festival, runner-up

2018, *The Widower,* Saints and Sinners: New Fiction From The Festival

2019, *Figlio Mio*, VIA: Voices in Italian Americana, 30.2

Acknowledgements:

After 30 years in education—encouraging and supporting writers, from children in elementary school, to young adults in pre-service teacher education, to veteran teachers taking in-service courses—I retired from teaching to focus on my writing, with the hope of having my work published. A challenging transition and an ambitious goal. There are many to whom I am grateful, but regarding the stories that appear in this collection, I thank editors Francine Ringold and Elis O'Neal of *Nimrod International Journal of Prose and Poetry*, the first to publish one of my short stories. I also thank Paul Willis and Amie Evans, editors of *Saints and Sinners: New Fiction from the Festival*, and the editors of *North American Review, VIA: Voices in Italian Americana, Gertrude Press*, and *Off The Rocks*. A special thank you to fellow writers at the 92Y, especially Leslie Michael Tabet, Anna Sabat, and Michael Serby for their generous input, and to Sue Weiss and Anne Marie Voutsinas, who are always willing to read my drafts. Author Joy Cohen recommended that I send my manuscript to Fomite, for that I am extremely grateful. Working with Fomite's Marc Estrin and Donna Bister has been a pleasure. I was thrilled that they accepted my collection for publication and greatly appreciated our respectful and transparent collaboration. Finally, thank you to Jack Stevens, my beloved partner of 39 years, who was more excited than I when my first story was published. He didn't get to read some of these stories, but writing them helped me through the early grieving years after he passed. And thank you to my son, Jesse, who (by example) teaches me that creating art takes persistence, dedication, and a lot of elbow grease.

About the Author

Vince Sgambati's debut novel, *Most Precious Blood*, was a Forward Indies Finalist in literary fiction, 2018, and a Central New York Book Awards Finalist. His short stories have been recognized by the Nimrod Literary Awards: the Katherine Anne Porter Prize for Fiction and the Saints and Sinners Fiction Contest (2013 & 2016). His fiction and creative nonfiction have appeared in *North American Review*, *Nimrod International Journal of Prose and Poetry*, *VIA: Voices in Italian Americana*, *Gertrude*, *Off The Rocks*, *Saints and Sinners: New Fiction from the Festival*, *Queer and Catholic*, *Journal of GLBT Family Studies*, and *Lavender Magazine*, where he wrote a regular column on Queer Parenting. Vince is a former teacher in urban public schools, long-time social justice activist, and currently makes his home in the Finger Lakes area of Central New York and in New York City.

For more information, visit https://www.vincesgambati.com/

About Fomite

A fomite is a medium capable of transmitting infectious organisms from one individual to another.

"The activity of art is based on the capacity of people to be infected by the feelings of others." Tolstoy, *What Is Art?*

Writing a review on Amazon, Good Reads, Shelfari, Library Thing or other social media sites for readers will help the progress of independent publishing. To submit a review, go to the book page on any of the sites and follow the links for reviews. Books from independent presses rely on reader-to-reader communications.

For more information or to order any of our books, visit:
http://www.fomitepress.com/our-books.html

More Titles from Fomite...

Novels
Joshua Amses — During This, Our Nadir
Joshua Amses — Ghatsr
Joshua Amses — Raven or Crow
Joshua Amses — The Moment Before an Injury
Jaysinh Birjepatel — Nothing Beside Remains
Jaysinh Birjepatel — The Good Muslim of Jackson Heights
David Brizer — Victor Rand
Paula Closson Buck — Summer on the Cold War Planet
Dan Chodorkoff — Loisaida
David Adams Cleveland — Time's Betrayal
Jaimee Wriston Colbert — Vanishing Acts
Roger Coleman — Skywreck Afternoons
Marc Estrin — Hyde
Marc Estrin — Kafka's Roach
Marc Estrin — Speckled Vanities
Zdravka Evtimova — In the Town of Joy and Peace
Zdravka Evtimova — Sinfonia Bulgarica
Daniel Forbes — Derail This Train Wreck
Greg Guma — Dons of Time
Richard Hawley — The Three Lives of Jonathan Force
Lamar Herrin — Father Figure
Michael Horner — Damage Control
Ron Jacobs — All the Sinners Saints
Ron Jacobs — Short Order Frame Up
Ron Jacobs — The Co-conspirator's Tale
Scott Archer Jones — And Throw Away the Skins
Scott Archer Jones — A Rising Tide of People Swept Away
Julie Justicz — Degrees of Difficulty
Maggie Kast — A Free Unsullied Land

Barry Goldensohn — The Listener Aspires to the Condition of Music
R. L. Green — When You Remember Deir Yassin
Gail Holst-Warhaft — Lucky Country
Raymond Luczak — A Babble of Objects
Kate Magill — Roadworthy Creature, Roadworthy Craft
Tony Magistrale — Entanglements
Gary Mesick — General Discharge
Andreas Nolte — Mascha: The Poems of Mascha Kaléko
Sherry Olson — Four-Way Stop
Brett Ortler — Lessons of the Dead
Aristea Papalexandrou/Philip Ramp — Μας προσπερνά/It's Overtaking Us
Janice Miller Potter — Meanwell
Janice Miller Potter — Thoreau's Umbrella
Philip Ramp — The Melancholy of a Life as the Joy of Living It Slowly Chills
Joseph D. Reich — A Case Study of Werewolves
Joseph D. Reich — Connecting the Dots to Shangrila
Joseph D. Reich — The Derivation of Cowboys and Indians
Joseph D. Reich — The Hole That Runs Through Utopia
Joseph D. Reich — The Housing Market
Kenneth Rosen and Richard Wilson — Gomorrah
Fred Rosenblum — Vietnumb
David Schein — My Murder and Other Local News
Harold Schweizer — Miriam's Book
Scott T. Starbuck — Carbonfish Blues
Scott T. Starbuck — Hawk on Wire
Scott T. Starbuck — Industrial Oz
Seth Steinzor — Among the Lost
Seth Steinzor — To Join the Lost
Susan Thomas — In the Sadness Museum
Susan Thomas — The Empty Notebook Interrogates Itself
Paolo Valesio/Todd Portnowitz — La Mezzanotte di Spoleto/Midnight
in Spoleto
Sharon Webster — Everyone Lives Here
Tony Whedon — The Tres Riches Heures
Tony Whedon — The Falkland Quartet
Claire Zoghb — Dispatches from Everest

Stories
Jay Boyer — Flight
L. M Brown — Treading the Uneven Road
Michael Cocchiarale — Here Is Ware
Michael Cocchiarale — Still Time
Neil Connelly — In the Wake of Our Vows
Catherine Zobal Dent — Unfinished Stories of Girls
Zdravka Evtimova —Carts and Other Stories
John Michael Flynn — Off to the Next Wherever
Derek Furr — Semitones
Derek Furr — Suite for Three Voices
Elizabeth Genovise — Where There Are Two or More
Andrei Guriuanu — Body of Work

Odd Birds

Plays

Essays